LUCIFER ON LEAVE

ROBERT LEE JOHNSTON

1

Also by Robert Lee Johnston:

Tribute

Tribute is a small, Australian township blessed with ancient mountainous rainforest, waterfalls, clean pristine rivers and a filthy secret. Six young lives are brought together by a church orphanage as wards of the state then groomed and sold off at a tender age. Other than the jungle, their only comfort is each other, and Stirrup, a brave blue cattle dog. The only family they have ever known.

Led by Cozy, wild, defiant and found in Tribute's rainforest as an infant, the youngsters plot the demise of their tormentor. Will the kids finally experience freedom and happiness? Or will tyranny and heartache stubbornly cling to them?

Refreshingly guttural and unashamedly Australian, Tribute's untamed growl is bold and confronting.

About the author

Robert Lee Johnston is an author based in Tropical Far North Queensland. He lives on a thirty-acre farm within the tropical embrace of Queensland's two tallest mountains. Alongside the farm a moody, cantankerous river winds its way into the coral sea.

Lucifer on Leave is his second novel.

www.robertleejohnston.net

ROBERT LEE JOHNSTON

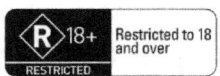 ROBERT + SCHOLTEN

If you are under age 18, or you arrived here by accident, please do not read further.

Lucifer on Leave
By Robert Lee Johnston
Copyright 2018 Robert Lee Johnston

Kindle Edition, Licence Notes

Cover by Robert Scholten
www.robertscholten.com

Paperback available at:
Amazon
www.robertleejohnston.net

For Wendy.

Everything.

MONTH ONE

Satan had been impatiently waiting a century.

The repetitive nature and daily grind of his work was oppressive and suffocating. The number of souls dispatched to him was always and ever increasing his workload.

Two or three recent wars hadn't helped maintain the status quo. He was restless and excited for the day to end. But, as in any large organisation, loose ends needed tying up and responsibility doled out to the most capable demons. It was a long, quarrelsome night in hell. Earth would come as a welcome relief for a year. Satan's annual day off work every century is equal to an earthly year. Each day in hell is a year here.

A church in the area of his centennial arrival would be forewarned and prepared for his visit with cash, clothes, and a brief rundown of the most recent times, trends and laws.

Of course, this deal was brokered with God's approval. The 'Big Man' and a reluctant 'Guardian of the Church', Archangel Michael, had created Ten Commandments to be obeyed. Never to be bent or broken by pain of terminating their agreement.

1 Thou shalt have no unnatural influence over man, woman or beast.

2 Thou shalt not reveal thy true self.

3 Thou shalt follow the rule of the land.

4 Thou shalt be given a vessel of my choosing.
5 Thou shalt feel.
6 Thou shalt be free.
7 Thou shalt have freedom of choice.
8 Thou shalt bleed.
9 Thou shalt be permitted onto hallowed ground.
10 Thou shalt not summon one thing from hell.

Every century since the beginning of time Satan has gone on leave for a day. Every century was a new adventure, a new country and a new taste of our evolving world.

This was his latest vacation.

The city he turned up in was hot and humid.

Even though it was night he was sweating and sticky. There was a strong ocean scent and, when he stumbled upon an Esplanade, a cool Pacific breeze greeted him.

He had landed in Cairns.

Australia.

He was met at a whitewashed, wooden church, simply constructed compared to Europe's ancient churches. He still carried a thick, old-English accent, a hangover from his last visit to Great Britain at the turn of the last century.

A priest, a humorous, happy, older man who had a local, out-of-tune voice with high-pitched, strange inflections, gave to him a new identification which read 'Lucian'. There was also cash, some credit cards and a house key.

It was 3 am on a Saturday when he left the wooden church. The local pubs and clubs were emptying as he wondered the streets with a mud map the priest had drawn for Lucian to find his house.

Five drunken local lads, nearly twenty years old and wearing blue jeans and various band-related T-shirts, flannies and old footy jerseys, approached from the opposite direction. They were loud and all over the shop, wrestling, laughing, mucking around, hunting for some rough-and-tumble.

'Check out what this bloke's wearing, boys!'

The lad's accent was strange to Lucian, loud, thick, laconic and, at first, affronting to his ear.

Lucian had been given clothes by the priest, clothes that the priest thought looked modern.

The tallest bloke looked to one of his smaller, stockier mates and spoke with a monotone voice. 'Jesus Christ, Ratty. Get a look at him. He's got MC Hammer's pants on.'

Lucian did! He had high-cut, bright-orange basketball shoes on each foot. His oversized, salmon-coloured parachute pants were pulled all the way up to his chest, accompanying a bright, gay, fluorescent yellow shirt with the word 'Funky' stencilled across its back, very baggy and very definitely from the eighties and out of whack.

'The wanker thinks he's Marky Mark, or Vanilla Bloody Ice,' another of the boys stirred.

They stared slack jawed at Lucian, and he felt a little anxious as the group staggered his way.

'Who the fuck do you think you are, dickhead?' the smaller, stockier one asked.

'One does not seek trouble from you good fellows,' Lucian pleaded kindly.

'Eh! He's got a pom jammed in his gob. Ha ha ha! One don't give a fuck what ya seek, ya poncy-talking poof,' one of the taller blokes said as he fumbled with his mobile phone, pointing it at Lucian then pressing record.

They blocked Lucian's path and wouldn't let him pass.

'Leave one to go about one's business and let one by.'

The lads bust a drunken gut with laughter at his response.

'And what are ya gunna do if we don't, ya pommie faggot? Eh?'

Lucian was speechless. Nobody at work dared ever confront him in this manner. Lucian felt something he hadn't felt in an age: pain.

One of the lads, punching wildly, attacked his head and then they all went for it. The melee made its way over the street to the darker side of the Esplanade. Like a ferocious cloud of swarming wasps, they all joined in the frenzy, punching and kicking Lucian to the ground.

Lucian, 'King of the Underworld', found himself in a foetal position upon the Esplanade's freshly mowed lawn, recorded on a drunken cameraman's mobile phone for prosperity and any interested YouTubers.

Then some bloke started ripping men off Lucian and tossing them away. When they landed on their feet they faced to attack again, only to stop in their tracks when they saw who it was. Beanz, a quiet fella who had lived in Cairns all his life. Beanz was one of the area's better footy players. A top bloke, but known for his meanness when provoked.

'You fellas dialled the wrong number.'

All the fight left the boys. Beanz chuckled to each of his teammates, telling them calmly, 'You boys are fucking mad, eh. Just go, Rat, quick. Take the boys with ya before the pigs show up 'n' lock us all up. Forget this galah.'

The group smiled.

'Man, we got a tough game tomorra' arv against those Yarrabah boys. Ya reckon them blokes are out fuckin' about and fighting, or sleeping getting ready to kick our arses?'

Rat was the team's hard-headed dummy half. Ratty was also versatile and volatile in his second role as hooker. When he started throwing punches he shut his eyes and ripped, hooked and upper-cutted, blindly taking them all on, often cleaning up one or two of his own players in the confusion. He laughed, dropping his aggression and flashing his broken hooker's teeth while telling his vice captain and prop, 'We were just headed home to get some sleep now, Beanz. Ya still playin' tomorra', bull?'

'Yeah, Ratty. I'll be having a run. I'm just having a light jog to loosen up me legs.'

'Awesome, big fulla!' Ratty was happy. 'Righto, catch ya then, bull.'

The pissed mob turned to leave, but not before Ratty told Lucian, 'Ya fucking lucky Beanz showed up, mate. Ya won't be so lucky next time, ya pommie dickhead!'

'Be gone ye hooligans!'

Lucian tried to sound intimidating. He was anything but. Beanz was a little surprised by the accent.

He had thought the stranger was an Aussie. Granted, a strange dressing one. But nothing about his face suggested a foreigner. He looked to Beanz like your typical corn beef, spud, cheese sauce and cauliflower-eating Aussie.

The other team members nodded and said goodbye to Beanz.

'C'ya boys.' Then Beanz asked as he helped Lucian up, 'Ya right, mate?'

On the deck, Lucian couldn't help but notice the size of his saviour's feet.

They were big feet! Like those of a Brisbane bloke. Beanz was well known for his feet. You'd have to skin a fully grown Murray Grey just to cover one foot. Beanz could easily slip those hooves of his into a pair of bull crocs and wear them as yard thongs. He offered his giant hand and Lucian took it.

Lucian was beaten up good. One hand cradled his face while the other touched, investigating random painful places. A tooth was missing, his eye swollen and his nose broken.

Beanz sucked in air through gritted teeth when he saw Lucian's busted nose. 'Ya' gunna need a bit o' calamine lotion I reckon, champ. I'm Beanz.'

'Lucian. Thank you, Beanz, for your assistance.'

'No worries, mate. Lucian, eh? I've never heard of a Lucian before … Shit, man, you know you're asking for trouble with a name like that 'round here? It's just ripe enough, that bloody name. You'll get plenty of sparring practice, bull! The locals'll have a ball with a name like that one. Ya better learn to fight a bit better if ya gunna call yourself Lucian in the pubs 'round here.

You know, like that boy named Sue Johnny Cash sings about? I'm gunna call you Luce. Just to be on the safe side, call yourself Luce while ya in Cairns, man.' Beanz had to ask the obvious. 'What the bloody hell are you wearing, Luce?'

'I just got given these I'm afraid. I have no garments other than these.'

Beanz did the math, adding the English accent and lost gear.

'You're a long way from Merry Old England, bull. Shit, did they lose ya luggage? Bloody airports, eh! They're fucking useless, aren't they?'

Luce didn't know what an airport was and changed the subject. He offered his face and crooked snout to Beanz. 'Please. Do you mind, my dear Beanz, straightening one's nose?'

There was a grin, a crunch and a grunt when one's bent nose was straightened.

'Thank you, Beanz.'

'No worries. Where are you staying, Luce?'

'At this abode.' He retrieved a key from his deep, baggy pocket with an address written on a blue plastic key ring. 'I only arrived a moment ago and have just now lost my map and bearings.'

Pain surged through him as he scanned the street for his sheet of paper. He hadn't felt that sensation for ten decades. It stung. The map had gone with the breeze.

'So this is ya first time in Australia?'

'Yes.'

'Bloody hell, that wasn't a real flash welcome, was it? All your gear lost. Then the local under-eighteen footy team kicking the shit out of you. Ya poor bastard.'

'One can only hope the trouble has abated for now.'

Beanz kind of liked the way he spoke. He had never heard anyone talk like that in real life. 'That's a hell of an accent you got there, Luce.'

'Thank you. Yours too is a very different strain of English.'

'Yeah, new people say that a lot up this way. I'll show you where your house is, Luce. It's not that far from here.'

They walked, and Beanz noticed blood on his hands. He got a good look at Luce's face under a street light.

'Shit, mate, let's get you to the hospital first, eh. Ya rougher than a punted pineapple and still leaking oil pretty bad. Your place is down past the hospital anyway.'

Luce had never in all his years been so confused by the language Beanz spoke, or seen such a thing as Cairns Base Hospital. Nurses were quick to assist him. The two nurses who cleaned and checked him over were sweet and well-rehearsed. A very busy, kind, young male doctor stitched and patched up an opened eyebrow and sent him on his way. Beanz waited patiently and then showed Luce to his home just off the end of the Esplanade.

'One must thank you for your assistance, Beanz.'

'Eh, no worries, mate. You know, you kinda remind me of someone? But I can't think who.' He thought about it. 'Hey, has anyone ever told you you look a bit like Bon?'

'No. I'm afraid this man, Bon, is unknown to me.'

'Bon Scott.'

'Doesn't ring a bell I'm afraid.'

'You never heard of Bon Scott? The singer?'

'Sorry, no.'

'You mean to say you've never heard of AC/DC or Angus Bloody Young?'

'Never.'

'Shit!' Beanz was a little stunned. Everyone he knew knew who Bon and Angus were. 'I dunno. You just look like you got a bit of mongrel in you, eh.'

It sounded to Luce's ears like: 'Idno. Yajus looklikeya gottabittamongrel in ya. A?'

'I reckon your messy hair and that fresh missing tooth of yours reminds me of him a bit. You sure you're right, Luce?'

'One should be fine, now home. Is he a handsome fellow, this mongrel singer, Bon Scott, of whom you speak?'

Beanz thought Luce was taking the piss and laughed. 'Women loved him and men wanted to be him. I guess he had something they wanted. Eh, look after yourself Luce and be safe, mate. Go inside, have a cup of tea, an aspro and a good lie-down. If I don't see you around, I'll see you through the window.'

Luce waved goodbye and smiled politely, not really knowing what Beanz meant.

His last night in hell was busy and his first here intense. In the house's darkness, Luce was impressed at the build quality of the home, even though he could find

15

no lamps or candles. There was carpet underfoot and food in the fridge. He marvelled at the light, God's eldest daughter, when she radiated from the fridge as he opened its door. He grinned, pleasantly surprised at the cold water and fresh food kept inside. It was then Luce caught a glimpse of his latest vessel in a kitchen window. It was a bit beaten up, but it was not an ugly man he was looking at. Rough, rugged, but not ugly. He was a young man, twenty-five-ish. This took a moment to adjust to. When you're as old as Lucifer, a young mortal, human body doesn't fit the reflection's equation. He was lean, sinewy, with thick, tangled, shoulder-length dark hair. His skin was pale and his teeth crooked. His tongue felt strange adjusting to his new mouth and its many shortcomings. Of course, he reached and looked inside his baggy, salmon-coloured trousers to feel and see his endowment.

Very average.

He washed his face gently with 'plumbed running water' for the first time in his life, and then lay for a moment on a comfortable bed. The house was quaint and clean, a little two-bedroom wooden house raised on knee-high stumps, with high ceilings and a great little verandah out front.

Luce needed light. Then there was light, when he fiddled with a toggle switch on the kitchen wall. Right next to the light switch hung a picture of Jesus with long brown hair that greeted him when darkness disappeared. There was very little, if any, likeness painted. Luce nodded slowly at the picture as he stared. Then he turned it around. There were many framed colourful butterflies of all sizes tastefully decorating the wall. And various paintings and sketches portraying outback Australian farm scenes, or the old settlers themselves. One or two pictures depicted snake and dingo dogs sleeping away on a wide, shady timber verandah under the corrugated-iron homesteads their masters had scratched out. Corrugated iron was a distinctive theme among the artwork. It was used for water tanks, feed troughs, walls, furniture ... almost everything. A few rustier examples sketched here and there showed the rotted-out remnants of what once were the homes of many pioneers and settlers. Forcing the observer to feel the harsh, palpable power of Australian time and the unforgiving nature of this country.

Luce grinned with pained lips as he read aloud an RH Croll quote framed amongst the art work.

When God knocked off one night, said He-
'This earth's a rotten failure;
How to improve it? Let me see ...'
Next day he made Australia.

Out the back door and down three missionary-brown-painted wooden stairs were the bathroom, laundry and toilet. Luce particularly loved the flushing toilet, deep claw-foot bath tub and running hot water. Man had moved faster than ever this last century. It took time to work everything out. He had cranked out two shits, squatting in the spacious backyard, wiping his arse with a fine-looking, smooth tropical palm leaf growing in the garden, plus half a dozen pisses out there against the next-door neighbour's fence before he figured out what the dunny was for.

Luce spent the better part of the next day discovering man's latest inventions. He found lots of white boxes that were in fact white goods. Washing machine, freezer, fridge etc. The television confused him so much he stood dumbfounded and wide eyed in front of it for half an hour before he blinked. Then he discovered on the coffee table a note from the twangy, banjo-voiced priest explaining how to turn it on, and everything else the house required.

As he read he felt an ancient, familiar presence.

Michael.

When he lifted his eyes from the note, there he was.

Silken, golden, downy wings that barely fit under the ceiling fan. Black haired, radiant, righteous, powerful and jaw-droopingly beautiful.

There was no love lost between the two. In fact, it never sat well with Michael that the deal was ever brokered. So, every century when Lucifer was on leave, he let Luce know that he was never far away.

Michael looked Luce over. No distinguishable feature was recognisable to his eye. Unremarkable in every way. His shape, his limbs, his body. His face held no trace of infinite wrath or that abominable fiend.

Luce growled. 'The Angel of Death. I was expecting you.'

Michael smiled a policeman's grin. 'That's just the way I like it, traitor.'

There was silence as both stared. Michael broke eye contact and looked around the tidy wooden room.

He walked to the reversed painting and hung it properly. 'Why must they always paint him this way?' he asked himself. He stood behind a two-seater lounge chair with his hands resting on its head rest. 'Not the palace you call home is it, powerless one? Comfortable, nonetheless.'

'Man truly has come far … my old friend.'

Michael was in no mood for him. 'I see you have made friends.'

He strode towards Luce, through the lounge chair, and touched Luce's swollen, blackened face. 'I love seeing you in this state. No power, no authority, and oh so fragile.'

The hatred and raw electricity between them was evident.

'I see you still belong to him. Still have my old crown. You are Michael, "like God", but you shall never be God.' Luce inhaled. 'So tiring it must be, forever the prince and never king … The middle ages were your best years, my old friend. You peaked far too early I'm afraid. And just once I wish you would come down and visit me, within my domain, upon my ground. You come to me now for you are a coward, Michael. If you came to me any other time, I'd devour you.'

'It is I who defeats you in the final hour! You have tried before and failed. You will fall again, in the end. How I await that day.'

Luce told the winged one, 'We all owe God a death. The final hour is far from now, Michael. The trumpet has not yet sounded. And yes, I am king.' Luce smiled at what he was about to say. 'What are you, nowadays, dearest Michael? Still ever the servant?'

'At the moment, dearest enemy, I am all powerful, and you a hollow, fallen, mortal shell.'

'Yes.' Luce nodded. 'Yes that is true. But there are rules, Michael. Rules even one as powerful as yourself must obey.'

'You will be seeing me, Lucifer.'

And he was gone.

Luce whispered to the emptiness, 'I believe you.'

Memories from the beginning of time stirred in Luce's mind and heart, bringing forth strong emotions and an aching within his head.

The Fifth Commandment was one of the most powerful of the ten.

Thou shall feel.

Guilt, shame, pride, envy, fear, anxiety, rage, obsession, hatred and his fall from grace pervaded his all too human emotions. All at once.

Adrenalin surged, filling his veins, creating a savage chemical headache. Luce raised his head and fists in the air and shook them angrily at God, remembering some words hurled at him along with that barrage of punches—'Ya poncy-talking poof!'—not really knowing what they meant. The pulsing, throbbing migraine worsened, and he raced to the toilet to vomit.

Michael left Luce alone for a while, and Luce learned how to live, communicate and get by. Mostly by watching television and listening in on conversations. He blended in very well and soon wandered around Cairns knowing where he was going. Of course, nobody but the happy priest had a clue they were co-existing and rubbing shoulders with the incognito Devil himself.

Food in past visits had always been an adventure by speedy dysentery, and that hell of all diseases, gut-wrenching food poisoning. Cairns, being so very multicultural, commanded a wide variety of familiar international flavours. Locally grown, in-season tropical fruits such as mangoes and lychees were, to his taste buds, divine. The fresh seafood and mud crabs were sweet, meaty decadence. Now and then he would raise his head to the heavens, concede, and smile at the perfection and taste of it all.

In a tiny store at the local markets, Luce found a picture with a poem to frame and hang on the inside of his dunny door. The picture was a drawing of a bloke squatting on the throne, pants around his ankles. Under the picture was written:

Here I sit broken hearted.
Tried to shit but only farted!

Luce got a good laugh out of that. One of his secret favourite things, when he visited earth as a human, was the pleasure of farting. A simple pleasure given to man, but a truly satisfying gift in a very elementary way. Another human trait he savoured was dreaming. He loved his human dreams. Luce's dreams, like ours, were uncontrollable, unpredictable, confusing, empowering, inspiring, disturbing and unimaginable. No rest for the wicked meant that on his own turf dreams were unheard of. You must first sleep to dream. And his hands, the Devil's, were never idle. Luce also didn't mind flicking channels at two in the morning to see a little SBS early-morning arse and ABC late-night titty. One of the most confronting sentences he ever heard on earth was on SBS at three or four in the morning watching, with an orchy-bottle bong and an ice-cold rumbo for company, some shitty European B-grade, subtitled movie. Two men, one wearing a brown paper bag with eye holes cut in it over his face and head, discovered the dead body of a pretty female teenager. The bloke wearing the paper bag turned to the other fella and asked really seriously in French, 'Do you think she's still warm?'

An unfortunate sentence.

Lastly and maybe most importantly, the pretty, free-spirited women in bikinis, swimming and relaxing on the Esplanade, were blowing his mortal mind. The women living in and visiting Cairns were purer than any art. Now and then Luce would catch himself staring or, even worse, be caught staring. Not in an evil, sexual or sinister way. He just found himself transfixed by a certain smile or style. The way, in particular, some women moved and were so at ease, confident of their looks and able to almost shift the air around them with mystery and beauty. Others, whose beauty lay deeper, mystified him with their shyness and not wanting to be noticed. He could see, through the eyes of his latest vessel, the depth of character and the sweet nature of some of these women. He had never witnessed so many colours, so much skin and so many beautiful ladies in one place. He smiled bright, glinting, broken teeth when a pretty young woman asked him something. His human heart would flutter against his ribs, and his mortal stomach grow anxious in their presence.

Afterwards, he would think of something much more articulate to say than the crap that spilled past his teeth.

Beauty intimidated him. Luce hadn't had much experience in that facet of life. He had missed beauty.

MONTH TWO

Luce was into week four of his holiday. He had purchased clothes that suited the current times. He found the garments trending in Queensland very comfortable and easy to manage. Luce had loved fishing on previous visits and stood gobsmacked under the roof of the local tackle and bait shop at the amount of fishing gear housed there. Being old school, he had purchased a hand line, some hooks and sinkers, and was going to dig up some worms from his backyard.

The assistant convinced Luce that a basic rod and egg-beater reel combo was worth a look into.

'If ya want a barra, use these.'

The assistant handed Luce a couple of 'Gold Bombers' and 'Bill's Bugs'.

'If one doesn't work, the other will.'

Luce was on the bank of the Barron River, around the slightest bend. Unknown to him, fifty yards away sat Beanz. He sat relaxing on his Esky, quietly, accurately casting away into the brown water, at an eddy, trying to snag himself a good brim that had shown some interest. He twisted open a round, patinated Log

Cabin tobacco tin with both hands and sparked into life one of the fat joints that were stashed inside. He toked on his joint and then sipped on a cold beer. The smell of his joint blowing downwind caught Luce's attention. He spied Beanz and recognised him. Beanz had a rather round, large face. Not fat or droopy skinned, just a big, wedge-like chunk of a head. His was a friendly face that could easily be mistaken for that of a daydreamer or someone fully removed from worry and strife. He had a lazy left eye, with slightly curly, corn-coloured hair always in his brown eyes. To some he appeared sleepy-stoned, happy-sleepy and mellow because his smile was always there or easily accessed. His voice was slow, calm and as deep as his shoulders. His bent nose had been broken at least once. But, thanks to cheap chemist mouthguards, his teeth were all intact. The large jaw that housed those teeth couldn't be broken with a tractor-driven pile driver. Six foot five and rising at seventeen, he was usually a giant slab of a wedged, chunky head above the rest. His fellow prop was a similar height, so when Rat/Ratty, their hooker and staunch middleman, all five feet of him, threw his arms over their necks and shoulders to pack into a scrum, Rat's feet would dangle as if they were hanging over a sheer cliff face when his props stood tall with him latched on. Ratty may have been short but he was three pick-axe handles broad, and that was just across his neck! His battered, harder than stone, hooker's head had three bold missing teeth. He was a wild boy, a wilder drinker, and both Ratty and Beanz were great thieves of the football. Loose or tight head, in a time when half backs feeding scrums, scrums, pack strength and hooking meant something. Forwards proudly PUSHED. Raking, head-butting, dominating, intimidating and punching the piss out of their opposite front rowers. Those efforts were the difference between winning and losing scrums, and a coach-pleasing scoreboard. Beanz lived for that manic, mob aggression bred inside a good, ole-fashioned, twelve-man competitive scrum.

Luce yelled up stream. 'Is that you, my old Beanz?'

'Who's that?'

Luce packed his gear up and made his way over the obstacles to see Beanz.

'Eh. Be buggered.' A little shocked, Beanz asked, 'Luce! How the hell are you, mate?'

'I'm good, I'm good. I just now saw a glimpse of your face and thought, he looks familiar. I never forget faces, you see.'

'Hey, I'm glad. How'd you pull up after that hiding you got?'

'All healed, one is happy to report. Wretched scoundrels! One must not underestimate the delight Australian males take in giving a stranger a smack in the head.'

Beanz laughed. He couldn't help but smile at the old English that Luce slipped in now and then. A comfortable, smiling moment passed, and Beanz found himself thinking how well Luce had healed. There was just a trace of the flogging he'd been dished out. He passed the joint to Luce.

Luce smiled. 'Ah, cannabis, the noble weed.'

'The Devil's Cabbage,' Beanz added.

Luce belly chuckled after he exhaled. 'The Devil's Cabbage, you say.' He nodded as he passed the joint back. 'I have never heard it called that before.'

'Where did you learn to speak the way you do, Luce?'

'Oh, here and there.'

'Oh yeah … where's that?'

'I come from an ancient family. Terribly, terribly rich you see, Beanz. Timeless, old money. My family has connections all over the world so we travelled and lived abroad a lot. I'm afraid I'm not quite up with your times.'

'Mate, you look and sound like you're picking it up. You're dressed much more like us natives today, and you seem to be picking up the slang pretty fast. How old are you, bull?'

Luce had purchased some T-shirts, shoes and denim jeans since they last met.

'I'm twenty-five.'

'Do you work?'

'I do. Terrifically mundane my work is. Numbers are my lot, sadly.'

'So you're an accountant?'

'Of sorts, yes. I'm centuries behind. Wars, you see; customers dying. In my line of expertise they tend to, regrettably, back numbers up. Though fortunately I'm having a year off. And I must admit, it feels like an age since I had a break.'

'Me too. I'm taking a year off before I go to university.' Beanz grinned at him. 'Good on you, Luce. Recharge the batteries, smell the roses and that.'

'Ah, university. What will you study, Beanz? And, "smell the roses?"'

'I'm not sure yet. And, you know, take some time off to enjoy the world and notice its beauty type thing? Do a spot of fishing. Smell the roses.'

Beanz took in a deep breath of fresh forest air.

'Oh, I see.' A moment passed. 'And so one shall take the time to smell the roses, as you suggest.' Luce took a deep draft of the sweet forest air.

'Whadaya reckon that is?' Beanz pointed to something oblong and blue just under the water's surface, casting distance from the forested bank they stood on.

'I can't say.' They both tried to decipher what they were seeing. 'It has one jiggered.'

'Same here. What the? Oh fuck! Luce, it's a kid!'

It was a naked baby, barely six months old. He was on his back, inches under the chilled, dirty water and almost impossible to recognise as human. The baby was blue as ink and very definitely a boy, for when the boy went through a shallower, stony rapid a rock lifted his belly and genitals to the surface momentarily.

Beanz threw his fishing rod aside and dove in, shoes and all. His large hand easily held the cold, lifeless lump.

The boy was deadly still.

A mother's scream from upstream broke the silence when she noticed her baby gone. Australia's vastness of space and ongoing emptiness can produce a scream so clear and shrill that the rivergums and paperbarks themselves shivered as birds of all manner scattered to the breeze.

Silently, the baby had crawled to the water's edge and slipped into its current.

Luce was climbing down the river's bank when Beanz grabbed hold of the kid on the other side of the river. The baby tumbled and was spanked by the rocky rapid he had just navigated. He was now in the calmer, deeper drop pool.

Beanz hurled the limp kid to Luce, who had been yelling into the forest, 'Your baby's found! Downstream, my lady!'

Beanz didn't want to hurt the kid, so tentatively threw him a little softer than he should have, splash landing him harmlessly two thirds of the way to Luce. Retrieving him after swimming he pegged the boy, hoping Luce would catch the messy tangle of lifeless, flying limbs. Luce easily caught him just as the boy's dad exploded out of the scrub like a startled deer, whiter than porcelain and eyes wide open. Luce lay the child on his back gently as his father pinched his nose and attempted to blow air into his tiny mouth. The baby's face and mouth were too small so the dad just covered both the baby's nose and mouth with his lips and forced oxygen in. The blue was fast turning into a misty grey before their eyes.

The whole world was silenced.

The child's little chest heaved with his father's breath but would not carry on of its own accord. After several attempts the mother arrived, shrieking as the father cursed Jesus Christ aloud.

So much time had elapsed.

The father drew a deep breath and arched like a bow as he did so, forcing so much air into his baby

Beanz thought the swollen boy would explode like a pin-pricked balloon. Luce and Beanz stole a glance and shook their heads remorsefully. The boy's mother fell helplessly to the ground, screaming … then the little bloke fired up.

'Little bugger just needed a bit of choke to get started,' Beanz said to nobody in particular, smiling. 'Just kicked into gear outta the blue.'

Luce agreed. 'What is this choke you speak of?'

Luce had never seen CPR performed and said to everybody amidst cries of joy, 'Splendid show, my good people.'

Mum went ballistic, shrieked some more and crushed the baby with hugs that would rival an old mumma grizzly. Then she turned her bear hugs on Beanz and Luce.

'Thank God you were both here. Thank God!'

You'd swear that Beanz and Luce had just given birth to that baby themselves by the look of relief and joy on their faces. Their goofy smiles were of disbelief and shock more than anything.

Luce wondered at just how the hell God got credit for saving the boy.

Dad sat on the ground, trying to catch his own breath and gather himself. He was shaking his head, in tears.

'I was just making lunch, a chicken bloody sandwich. I looked away, got distracted. Oh man!'

'It's okay, bull,' Beanz reassured him.

Dad was mid twenties, fresh faced and clean shaven, a solid, fit-looking bloke with a tattoo here and there.

'Shit, if you two weren't here.' He shuddered.

He told the boys his name and he remembered theirs. He got up and shook both their hands, telling them thank you, thank you. His wife had settled enough to come over and introduce herself and thank the boys again. He was a good bloke and she seemed cool. They admitted to the boys that the child was still to receive a middle name, and between Luce and Beanz they would come up with a middle name to honour them both. They quickly said their goodbyes to the boys as they needed to get their baby to a doctor straightaway to make sure bub was okay.

'Amazing wasn't it, when the boy woke up?' Luce exclaimed to Beanz.

'Thank fuck all right.'

Neither's heart was into fishing anymore and they silently packed up their gear. As they walked through the forest the lads discussed what would have happened if they weren't there.

'I thought he was fucked there for a while. He was blue eh, Luce? He was dead for a bit there, mate. We saved his life, I reckon.' Luce agreed. They dwelled on that thought for a time.

Beanz asked, 'Don't you get a free pass? Sorta immune from bad shit if you save someone?'

'That sounds fair, one would assume.' Luce could see where Beanz was going with the thought.

'I could run amok and be guaranteed no repercussions, right?'

'Who knows how such things work?' Luce commented with a grin.

31

The track was getting steep so nothing was said for a while.

'Ya reckon that little fulla knew what was going on, Luce?'

'For his sake, one hopes not. There are exceptions, of course, but, in general, the consciousness does not develop until around the age of three.'

Beanz wondered how Luce had gained this knowledge for odd facts, or whether he was just full of shit.

'I'd hate to drown, man. I remember when I was a kid, I jumped into this lake and sank like a stone. It was really deep. And cos I didn't know I was drowning it was pretty cool; you know, quiet and peaceful. Until I needed to breathe, then things got loud and violent, if only in my head.'

'Who saved you?'

'Me old man, eh. He dove in and found me like a rock stuck to the bottom. He reckoned I was pretty happy to see him. I don't reckon what they say about drowning is true, you know, it being like a dream.'

'Me either. Fuck drowning and fuck choking.' Luce had been there. He was fast learning the lingo.

Beanz asked, 'What's the go with these blokes choking themselves while they have a wank? Fuck dying with ya knob in ya hand. They reckon the closer to death you are the more intense the orgasm.' Beanz thought about that. 'Well, by that logic a ninety-six-year-old bloke must be blowing lava chunks! Like one of those massive travelling irrigators.' Beanz laughed out loud. 'Don't wanna drown, don't wanna choke, don't wanna burn. What's a good way to die, Luce?'

'Quickly and quietly.'

'Fuck that, bull! When I go I'm going kicking and screaming, all the way. I'll whinge, moan and bitch till my very last breath. How blue was that kid, man? It was like the other side of blue, grey-blue. Yeah, he was grey all right! Zombie grey. You reckon he might be ... bit fucked up after that?'

'What on earth do you mean, Beanz?'

'You know, he might be a vegetable, a cactus, fucking brain dead now.'

'One hopes not, Beanz. I would rather death.'

God had pulled the cabbage-and-eggplant card on Luce one time in the past. The memory of losing one's self like that, perfectly trapped inside an unresponsive body, frightened Luce.

'Yeah. I bloody hope that little rooster is okay. I didn't think he was waking up.'

Using the vernacular badly Luce said, 'One shat a brick.'

Beanz giggled at the attempt. 'Good try, mate,' he assured him.

The young blokes drove Beanz's second-hand, green, 1972 six-cylinder Cortina back to town. Luce had walked to the Barron River's forest. It took most of the morning. He had never been in a car. He panicked when it shot off.

Beanz needed to see it straight.

'So I can be bad as I want now, and nothing will happen, cos I saved that rug rat?'

'I'm not sure how that all works.'

Beanz had never been to a church once in his life, so God alone knew how he came to that conclusion.

Beanz asked, 'But what if I accidentally kill someone?'

'Beanz, you can do whatever you want, if you want. You have the power of choice.'

Beanz would soon feel that everything seemed to happen more intensely around Luce. People would get their noses out of joint about nothing in particular when he was close to them. Men would get upset and yell at their women. Lightning struck nearer to him. Solid, unshakeable things toppled. Rivers of water moved with violence around him. Drowned babies floated by in his presence! If the sun was shining it seemed brighter, hotter, nearer. Brewing storm clouds seemed darker, moodier and closer. Mother Nature was uneasy in Luce's company. Beanz thought that was pretty cool as there was never a dull moment. What happened in his eighteenth year would shape the rest of his life. Saving a soul almost certainly cost Beanz his.

Beanz was on a roll. He was stronger than he thought. He figured that maybe knowing Luce emboldened him to be himself. Perhaps that is what a good friend does, he thought. They give you strength to be yourself. Beanz told nobody about saving the child. He believed if he did the good fortune earned may fail and fold. A few months later, Beanz helped stabilise a fellow student who suffered a metal lathe accident, stemming the bleeding till help arrived, doubling his prize.

Beanz was simple minded but very far from stupid. He took people at face value, here and now. He wasn't interested in how rich or poor people were. He didn't care where a bloke came from. Beanz was a hard man to get along with. He despised dickheads and morons. He was sure the older he got, the more fools he met. He was a big bloke for his age, and, living in Far North Queensland, any time a footy jersey was thrown onto his back it was that of a prop forward. On the field he was tough as wood, explosive and could blast teams' defences wide open. Beanz kept to himself and was very independent. Some people act and talk tough and underneath their bravado lies a conniving coward. Beanz was the opposite. He was quiet and a little shy but when provoked he would devour men like a speeding train running through a mob of red kangaroos.

Luce didn't bore Beanz or want mindless, petty things from him. Luce seemed cool to Beanz. Well spoken, mysterious, funny. Just strange enough, and not at all needy. His sense of humour was old fashioned but spot on. It was a colder, drier sense of humour, Beanz found himself thinking.

Luce thought Beanz was great company and 'a bloody ripper'. Quintessentially Australian, humorous, humble, staunch and stoic. He was a broad-shouldered, thick-legged bloke, mature above his years. His thoughtful mind calm, sharp and loose. He possessed a flexible, slightly twisted sense of humour.

Neither of them realised it then, but they were soon to become good mates.

MONTH THREE

'Look at the flies on Paris, Beanz.'

They both took a gander at Luce's immediate neighbour.

Luce continued, 'Only a true five-star piece of shit could attract that many.'

'He's such a dead-shit I reckon he's about the only bloke in Australia a sack of angel dust would give some personality.'

They both stared at Paris through their wraparound sunnies.

A large, bold, vertically challenged, tropical, Far North Queensland sun was bright and close enough to weld with, so dark sunglasses are standard equipment around here all year long.

'How the fuck he gets laid is beyond me.'

'You're forgetting, Luce. He only fucks the women nobody else wants to.'

'Yeah, but that's still more pussy than I'm getting.'

'Ya don't wanna be going where he goes, mate. You're better off dry than going anywhere near those hags he roots.'

They both laughed as they remembered a few of the stray, horny, hungry hippos leaving the morning after he bedded them.

Luce and Beanz had known each other a couple of months, and Luce's English accent was a thing of the past.

He was truly a local-sounding bloke.

Luce told Beanz, 'Isn't it curious how those skinny, littler blokes love the big girls.'

They were sitting on Luce's spacious, shady front verandah when the 'hippo slayer' fired up his lawn mower.

Paris was a cheap, despotic, euro-trash-talking Bananastanie from some broken-down, tyrannical, backwater, shitty dictatorship. His younger brother, Milan, bought the house next to him. He was even worse. Beanz reckoned that they both should stop soaking their tampons in vinegar before inserting them into their sour orifices. Both were unassimilated, cowardly, rude, abrupt, anti-Semitic and antisocial, with a taste for dictating to their immediate street and community.

Both had poofy-sounding first names. Luce said, 'I'd hunt my old man down if he called me anything like that. May as well have called him, "Milan loves it up the bloody rudder"!'

'Does he know he's gay?' Beanz asked while watching Paris mow shirtless in his red speedos.

'He will be the last one to find out, mate.'

'I bet his ancestors were chased with muck-rakes and pitchforks from the hills and caves they called home by a mob of angry, disgruntled peasants.'

Luce smiled a robber's grin. 'I can barely understand a word he says. I wanna tell him that the grunts he comes out with are good for fuck all here. "Fuck you, I shoot you, fucking. I kill you, bloody!" are about the only English he has nailed.'

Beanz imitated sensationally a teary Sandra Sully, the news reader. 'On a final note we, as a nation, would like to give our heartfelt thanks to Paris 'n' fuckin' Milan's parents.' There was a solemn pause. 'Today, scientific communities around the world gather in confusion and delight, to question the miracle that is the latest jigsaw piece discovered within human evolution. The question must now be answered: How exactly do a monkey's arse and a stick insect conceive two human sons? These new, stunning revelations are beyond even Charles Darwin's wildest imagination.'

On a good day Beanz wanted to kick them. Much more on a bad day. The mongrels were about as smooth as bathtub bourbon or sour milk. They annoyed the shit out of all their neighbours with their sticky beaks and authoritarian attitudes. One by one they all tired till they were loath to even mention their names. 'Paris fuckin' Milan.' Slowly drove them all to drink. Now and then the cooler neighbours would pull up and have a chat amongst themselves, and sometimes they shared their latest run ins. 'Ya wouldn't believe what I saw those fucking idiots up to the other day!' Or, 'Did yas hear?'

One neighbour, Bruce, spoke to Luce recently. He passed on the gossip to Beanz over a couple of hungover lunchtime meat pies and strawberry milks. 'Did you hear he kicked the missus out.'

'Yeah, I heard.'

'Did you hear he's moved his daughter's best mate in?'

'No … As a tenant or something?' Beanz was cradling a sensitive temple with one hand and eating with the other.

'No, man, into his bed.'

Beanz choked on the pie's lighter pastry when, mid bite, he breathed in at the news. He was all questions and coughs.

'What sorta bloke?'

'I dunno.'

'That's quasi-incestuous, isn't it?'

Luce told him, 'Shit yeah. No matter where you come from, that's pretty crook.'

'Jesus! Was he grooming her as a kid?'

'I dunno.'

'How old is the daughter?'

'I dunno.'

It was a lot to absorb.

Beanz asked, 'Oh fuck! Was she a kid when he met her?'

'Hope not. Shit, man, I can't help but wonder now, bloke.'

Beanz flicked some corn-yellow hair from his eyes. 'That's fucking sick, man. I can see it, bull! I bet he was one of those dads that slaps his daughter's friends on the arse with the missus sitting right there, then says shit like, "How are young females going, fucking bloody?" With his big ole pot gut, half a mongrel inside them bright, tight, red budgie smugglers and those skinny, hairy little spider insteps poking out of 'em.'

39

They both cracked up laughing and looked on at Paris with newfound horrified eyes.

'Bruce, he reckons ole mate Paris is going to marry her.'

For the second time in as many minutes Beanz choked. 'What? This shit just gets sicker by the fucking second. Seriously?'

'True shit, mate. '

'Sick fuck ... So you're telling me that hairy, puny, sack of shit is marrying his daughter's best friend?'

Luce took a moment to let that question just hang there. 'Yep. True as I'm standing here.'

'You wouldn't dream this shit up in a thousand years.' Beanz paused. 'Sounds rapely, eh!'

'Not wrong.'

'I feel dirty just hearing it.'

'Me too,' Luce added. 'Quasi-incestuous is piss funny, mate.'

'What do you reckon her parents said, Luce?'

'Fuck knows. Poor buggers must be homicidal.'

Beanz looked at his pie.

'Shit! I can't eat another bite after hearing that.'

They were both badly hungover. Beanz removed his sunnies, shook the annoying hair from his brow and asked Luce, opening an eyelid with thumb and forefinger, 'Is there even an eyeball in this socket?'

'Yes. A bright red one with cactus thorns all up in it.' Luce got to thinking. 'You reckon the daughter and her friend are still mates?'

'Shit, bull, so when they get married, the daughter's friend will be her step mum. Is that right? It sounds wrong.'

'That's right. It's a head-fuck!'

Beanz smiled. 'I give 'em three months, tops.'

The cops arrived to warn Beanz for antagonising the coward nark Paris. They both had been waiting. Beanz had made a sign out of an old bit of corrugated iron and two rusty star pickets that held a phrase he overheard a tourist tell the publican once: 'Paris and Milan are quite gay.'

The tourist was, of course, talking of Europe: 'Gay Paris.' 'Gay Milan.'

'I love the cities Paris and Milan, that's what the sign says,' Beanz pleaded. The cops didn't buy it. Paris was trying to get his two cents in while the police were present.

'I no-a like-a sign, a bloody.'

Beanz told him, 'Fuck you, Paris.'

'Fuck-a me? Fuck-a you!'

'Learn English, ya Euro trash, quasi-incestuous piece of shit.'

Everyone within earshot almost pissed themselves as their new nicknames were coined. Good ole 'Gay Paree and Gay Mee-larn' was what people around town called them now. Thick, laconic, Far North Queensland accents trying to speak Anglo/Slav/French, noses turned up, lips tightened.

'I bump ped in tooo mis'sure Gay Paree why just this morn-ning, ma-ate.'

Of course, only behind their backs. Some who had no tact and little time for the two-man regime said it to their faces. 'Ya know we all call you blokes gay?'

It was fast getting politically correct around Cairns. If a bloke were to call someone gay or a faggot nowadays the police would spring into fast, furious action … much faster than the monthly threat of Paris fuckin' Milan shooting everybody on the street. The scary part was that both of them owned rifles, and, being those special kinds of pelicans, they wielded them. When armed fools lose arguments, sabres and rifles tend to be rattled. Now and again a neighbour would be rudely woken or overhear one of the other neighbours—who had just had a loaded semi-automatic .22 or an old 303 pulled out on them—yell out and warn them, 'PARIS FUCKIN' MILAN, put those fucking rifles away before I snap 'em and shove them up both your arses!'

There were headlocks, choke-holds, blood and fisticuffs. Only when their numbers were superior did they ever shape up. If they were alone, one on one, mano-a-stickinsecto, they would tool up with hockey sticks, bats and rifles. Essentially, Paris fuckin' Milan were big-mouthed, big-noting, gammon, spineless cowards.

Another neighbour, Pud, was sitting around a raging backyard fire slash barbecue with a mess of ravaged forty-pounder rum bottles and passed-out footy players. Pud was in his mid forties and was holding a party at his place for the team's most recent victory. He invited the hard-drinking team and his cooler neighbourhood friends along. That was where and when a humbled Turtle, Ratty and the boys politely apologised to Luce for giving him that touch up on the Esplanade. Luce told them, 'No worries, boys,' and all was sweet between them. Pud was the local under-sixteens coach, a no-nonsense, mean-talking sort of bloke with a rusty horseshoe moustache. He told Luce, Beanz, and the hardiest of players and drunken devils still standing, pissed as farts, as they passed tasty, fat joints in a clockwise direction, 'If those two bastards ever ended up in prison, I reckon by the time those two cock-sucking wankers got out, neither of those big mouths would have a gag reflex to worry about anymore!' He shook his head. 'The hard arses locked up in that joint wouldn't take their shit for one second. They would bash them, then fuck the guts 'n' face outta 'n' offa those two savages. Ya wouldn't wanna kick one of them brothers up the arse, mate! Ya foot would catch the Paris-Fucking-Milan herp. You can't never wash that shit off, boys.' He went on proudly, 'And, by the way, yous'll never hear me call 'em bloody Gay Paris or Gay Milan. Or Paris fuckin' Milan. I call 'em Paris-Fucking-Milan. Cos I reckon, Paris has fucked Milan. Done the dog with him. He's gotta of fucked his little brother at least once, eh boys? You know, just so he could see how it felt!' He grinned cheeky teeth after having a huge toke. Blowing out the smoke, he told the lads, 'I bet that's what Paris told his mum.' He paused for effect. 'When she opened the tool-shed door and found Milan, grimacing, bent over the Old Victa, moaning. Up to his guts in his brother's nuts.'

'You fucking know it!' Luce told him, throwing his head back in laughter.

'Christ, Luce. You've seen him, eh, Beanz? He's an animal, and he's fucked everything else that had a breath left in it.'

Ratty and Beanz told the others about a moment in the game. Ratty started by saying, 'He was a cheeky, quick-witted bastard that prop of theirs, eh Beanz?'

Beanz agreed. 'Did ya hear what the prick asked me?'

'Yeah.' Ratty laughed. And some of the others wanted to know what was said.

'I was hangin' off Beanz getting ready to pack in when the bloke opposite Beanz asked him, "Do you believe twins can sense one another and feel one another's trauma when there's distance between them?" Old Beanz was a bit stumped by the left-of-centre question and goes, "Yeah, I guess." Quick as ya like the fella asks Beanz. "So does that mean when Big Foot has worms you get an itchy arse?" "Hell-fuckin'-lo!" I yelled, as I unhooked from Beanz and punched that fucker!'

The drunkards all laughed then reminded a swaying Turtle of when he thought Paris fuckin' Milan had violated his arsehole. Or, worse, Ratty skewering him! Some of the wilder footy teammates had just recently moved into a share house. Half a dozen young blokes, all fresh out of the nest with no mums around to clean up after them, spending far too much personal time and intimate space with mates in the same tiny, carefree, grubby abode. That house was always good fun to visit and the boys were great value, but it put Beanz off his tucker. He saw in that house a large dog, standing on its back legs, its front paws and elbows comfortably resting on the dining table, licking milk out of a shared breakfast cereal bowl at the table with its hungover owner. Never once did he see a bowl especially for the dish licker. It ate food off the same plates as its master, or the bare floor. Beanz had seen footy blokes and their girlfriends answer the door of that house starkers, refusing to wear clothes while indoors, sitting around, sweaty-balled and bare-arsed, on communal furniture. One time only he stayed the night with them. After having a big win on the field, the boys partied and drank till the wee hours. Beanz, too pissed to leave, fell asleep exhausted on the couch, under a proudly framed, coveted poster of King Wally, next to a couple of mud-stained dirt bikes dripping oil, leaning against the wall of the living room.

Turtle screaming RAPE had woken the whole house up. The boys had fucked with him royally while he was sleeping. Taking an old classic and customising it for Turtle. Beanz and the lads decided to spit in a condom, each taking turns to fill it halfway up with saliva. Then Ratty opened a jar of vegemite and ran a fingertip through it and wiped a little of it on the outside of the condom. The lads burst out laughing when Ratty put the vegemite down and picked up a bottle of tomato sauce and squirted a dollop onto the franger. Then he smeared the sauce and vegemite together with his fingers, creating a comprehensively convincing sperm-filled, shitty-looking prop, deciding a pinch of chili pepper would create a genuinely authentic 'hot dot'. Earlier in the night they had found Turtle crashed out, fried, snoring in the backyard on his guts, sprawled out, with only jocks on. They hurriedly plotted, and then somebody fetched a wooden spoon, because nobody wanted to use a finger. Giggling and shushing each other they peeled his jocks aside, and, with the handle of the spoon, wedged home the condom soundly between his hairy cheeks, finally returning his jocks to their original position. They had decided not to tie a knot in the condom, for authenticity's sake, so several discoloured varieties of saliva were already amalgamating, leaking and dripping sinfully out of it, drying into Turtle's undies and sticking to his furry ring-gear. When Turtle got up, badly sunburnt, at around 11 am, he took a piss in the backyard and, with his dick in one hand, scratched his arse good morning with the other. He noticed a bit of irritation and acutely hot discomfort on and around his freckle. He felt something foreign, sloppy and slippery in his undies, so he fished around in the back of his jocks for it. Nobody saw the face he made when a used, blood-and-shit-stained condom appeared in his hand when the thin-ribbed rubber, with a tug, snapped free from his clammy, white, hairy arse crack. But they bet it was a bloody ripper.

Turtle screamed RAPE and the whole household chuckled, remembering what they had done to him in the earlier hours. Turtle was pissed off—really pissed off—and wanted to know who had fucked him! He reckoned, 'You bastards. Fuck yous. Yas have all gone too far this time!' It took ages for the lads to admit to Turtle what had actually happened. In the meantime they told him, 'You musta got diddled by some old, unwashed homeless fuck wandering by.'

'Paris fuckin' Milan, they mighta got hold of ya, mate!'

Ratty told him, 'Shit, Turtle. Ya got me worried. I'm a huge cummer, eh. How much jism was in that franger?' All the boys had seen Rat's hammer proudly displayed in the dressing-room sheds. A hippo would be proud of that appendage. Turtle yelped, 'NO!' He pointed to Ratty's groin. 'NOT THAT FUCKING THING! Fuck ya, Ratty. It was halfway full, ya bastard! No fuckin' wonder me arse is burnin'.'

'I'm sorry, Turtle.' Ratty looked doe eyed and guilty. 'I was pretty pissed last night and got a hard-on or a piss-fat there for a bit. I think, maybe, it was me, Turtle? But I don't remember rootin' ya!'

On and on it went.

When Beanz woke to Turtle yelling rape that morning his face was stuck firmly to the lounge chair's cool vinyl with old drool. His face peeled off the sofa's rankness like an old fridge sticker. He wiped his chin on his shirt front, and then was coldly greeted by a fantastic hangover, and a rash down the left side of his face and body, along with an annoyingly unrelenting itchy ring. To top it off he had also contracted through the night a healthy dose of pink eye in his left eye. 'I think I have got Big Foot's worms, cos my arse is itching so much,' he told Ratty. But they couldn't tell if he was itchy and pink-eyed because of the dog hair, bed bugs, gut worms, or faecal matter from the free-balling, bare-arsed occupants. A combination of all three had not escaped their minds. Beanz then noticed old, discarded, yellowing toe nails scattered willy-nilly over the coffee table. Turtle, the team's smallest player, could easily stuff his toes into his mouth, contorting his legs and back, chewing at and tearing shards of blackened, unwashed toe nail off with his bare teeth, and then spitting the remnants onto the table, towards housemates, or any target, with uncanny accuracy. Beer cans, many, many XXXX cans with a hot mouthful or two left, stewing discarded cigarette butts and trapping flies inside them, decorated the house, waiting to ambush some poor bugger who mistook one of those warm ash-tray-tin fly traps for their cold, fresh beer. Beanz saw floors so dirty in that house he wiped his feet to go outside. Once, while they were on a bender, Beanz had taken the lid off a pot simmering away forgotten on the stove for a look see. Inside was dire: a watery gruel the colour and consistency of dirty sock fluid awaited the hungry. A poor imitation of food. He could smell beer in there and recognised baked beans, spaghetti, champignons, some sunken, whole, unwashed potatoes. Milk or perhaps yogurt had also been introduced. The holy trinity—barbecue, Worcestershire, and tomato sauce—had been thrown in for flavour along with a tin of minestrone soup, with what appeared to be tinned sardines or herrings swimming about, keeping a couple of whole gherkins and black olives company. It smelt horrific, and Beanz couldn't place the odour that greeted him, or even identify a few of its more offensive ingredients. It seemed to Beanz that each of the lads, at one stage or another, had walked by the pot and added their own distinctive touch with whatever was within reach, and then left it forgotten. Dishes and cutlery, unwashed, could almost walk, like the hammers in the Pink Floyd music video, to the backyard for their monthly hosing down with a high-pressure Karcher high pressure cleaner. Six eighteen-year-old Aussie fellas and all their transient mates and girlfriends under one roof, at the same time, was the closest thing to a perceivable missing link that modern man had ever witnessed.

Beanz would find time now and then to contemplate his newfound friend.

Recently he was laid up, badly hurt and staying at home in his parents' old two-storey Queenslander. Beanz had accidentally knocked his grandfather's competition axe head off a work bench in the back shed after stropping and oiling it. His granddad, even in old age, was more than handy with it when he was alive. In his prime he was winning events around the district at the local rural shows. The wood chops.

In the beginning, way back when, capable, calloused timber men, their diligent wives, fellow pioneers and hardened settlers, coined a common, widely used stanza, lionising their earnest and most difficult of inaugurations and initiations to the Virginal Deep North of Australia. The stanza was perhaps, arguably, the very earliest, original, verbally recorded measure of an Australian national anthem in living memory.

If it moves, shoot it.
If it doesn't, chop it down.

Those crafty, cunning timber men, back then, would suddenly appear from the scrub, unshaved and wily as goldfield Chinamen, a staunch, lean jungle dog at their sides and their latest, greatest axe head sharpened to a scalpel and polished brilliant till it shone like a mirror within its appropriated hardwood axe-carrying box. On competition days these blokes perpetually had in one hand a cold stubby, in the other their hottest axe, with a half-smoked, rough-cut, perfectly rolled rollie casually hanging out one corner of their tight-lipped gobs.

This particular axe head was a fiddly, easily blunted, specialised, high-performance piece.

It was revered. To the extent that a covetous grandson's stolen glance at it would be to knowingly court the Devil himself. It was a child and his co-operatives' Kangaroo Court death sentence to open the hardwood, heavy-hinged box to see the thick, soft, red-and-black flannel material the axe resided in.

A boy 'n' his mates could, by an unwritten law, be shot, beaten and/or strangled to death on sight.

No shame.

No warnings.

No hesitation.

No explanation.

No apologies.

No guilt.

Not even a shallow grave would be dug if the grandson and his mates, who ought not to have, were holding 'me bloody racin' axe!' Let alone chopping a block into splinters. If you wanted to see an old man's blood instantly broil his eyes dry as if he'd just been handed a cold pie and a warm beer, try chopping dry firewood on a hardwood stump with it with some blokes you know. A long, sturdy-handled 'beating shovel' would magically appear in the old man's calloused hands if the aforementioned boy/children/mates merely daydreamed or fantasised about touching it. Not to bury them with, no, but to smack them over and over the head with until rendered dead. The unapologetic attending police officer wouldn't bat an eyelid. He would casually and disdainfully kick the villainous carcass/carcasses to make sure they were sufficiently and satisfactorily dead. Sympathising with and understanding perfectly the absolute necessity for the owner of such a fine, beautiful axe and perfectly designed handle to shoot, beat and throttle the life out of that stupid, thoughtless, disrespectful boy child and those dopey, shoulda-fuckn'-well-known-better mates of his.

In Beanz's mind this axe was a beast, a natural extension of his grandfather's body. Woodchopping wasn't like the sport is today. There was no money or anything for the champion other than being tickled pink by a tiny medallion, and then owning the most valuable blue-chip bragging rights for a year. Christ, they were tough men, and scared of nothing. Men today can't possibly consider themselves comparable to that particular evolutionary strain of human. Their Darwinian existence and the traits inherited from surviving those hardships have been lost to modern man-dom. They felled timber, clearing this land with bullock teams by hand for a living. Then went to the wood chops to chop timber, for fun and sport! It was almost impossible to make that variety of human cry. Beanz once, and only once, saw his grandfather's eye spill a tear, when recalling the death of his eldest daughter. Those men, Homo non-cryus, held every crying emotion in their jaws' ligaments, tensing them so hard their skull muscles twitched around their temples. Trembling lips were the only tell that they were close to falling apart.

Chainsaws were not around during those early times. Wars, bullocks, beasts of burden, cross saws, bullwhips, blood, fire, muscle, sawmill pits, endurance, grit and axes were the order of the day for felling scrub and opening up the far north's country. They were wiry, dangerous, sinewy men who lived solely on rough-cut tobacco, billies of black tea, cast-iron camp ovens and flour for damper. Courser and tougher than a tramp's foot, they knew every inch of their forest and mountains. Each water source and hunting trail. And, of course, when a bloke was dry, he knew the fastest route to the nearest pub, for a coldie, from any point on the map.

Not at all like the Paul Bunyon-looking blokes that are produced professionally today. These particular men disappeared into the forest for nine months of the year and on their return performed, in a time-honoured fashion, 'The List.'

One.

Give the boys a wicked hiding for all the bad things they done but didn't get caught for in their father's absence.

Two.

Kick that mangy house mutt hard right in the guts for all the bad things it done but didn't get caught for in his master's absence.

Three.

Meet the newest baby.

Four.

Stuff another baby in the missus.

Five.

Drink the pub dry. Fighting whomever or whatever may challenge, all wet season.

Doing it all over again once the wet cleared off. Hardened men surviving in crude, mozzie-plagued camps, lit by hurricane lamps, barely fit for hogs while they toiled timber.

As the axe head fell, Beanz didn't want to see the blade damaged or chipped by striking the shed's concrete-slabbed floor. He saw and heard in his mind's eye for a moment his grandfather, with a large-handled shovel appearing in his old busted paws. 'Me bloody racin' axe!'

It was a reflex really. Under his imagined grandfather's gaze, Beanz stuck his foot out to break the shiny, heavy, razor-sharp axe head's fall. It fell deeply into his thonged foot and thumped in solid when it broke through the bone and the thong's two thin rubber straps. His foot had his face's wide-eyed amazed reflection shining up at him off the cold steel. It bit like a grinder's cutting wheel being dragged across the top of his foot. The pain that sung to him took a moment to realise itself, and he thought, Righto. It's okay. It doesn't hurt that bad. Then it hurt something chronic! Beanz wasn't sure if he yelled or yelped. Flesh, pain receptors, veins, nerves and tendons screaming overwhelmed him. The symphony of agony deafened Beanz momentarily. The mirror-finished cutting tool was lodged atop his foot like a half-cocked guillotine blade. Beanz's foot weighed a tonne and it flapped a bit, like a busted shoe tread. He noticed a lot of blood. Beanz was going to instinctively pull it out when he remembered hearing something about leaving things like that well alone. Being an Aussie kid, he thought he would make the most of his current situation. He called out as calmly and nonchalantly as possible from the shed to his mum. 'Hey, Mum!'

'What, love?' came her call.

'You'll never guess what just bit me. Come downstairs and have a look.'

'Righto. Give us a sec.' She stopped what she was doing and made her way down the steps to the shed. 'Did that big red-back bite ya on ya bum, did it?' She giggled out loud when she got to the shed's door. 'I told you it would get ya!' She smiled at Beanz. 'Where did ya get bit?' Her eyes focused, and then sweetly squinted, and like a bird of prey she scanned her son. Beanz pointed to his foot. His dear old tender-hearted mum looked down and her eyeballs, at first, rolled topside in her head. Then the whites turned into the heavy red eyes of a stoner and, as usual, she made her way to the ground, like a preacher slowly falling to her knees. She passed out. Didn't like the sight of blood one bit did Beanz's mum. Even the mention of blood made her light headed. If Beanz explained or described an injury, or even said the word maggots, he could make her dry retch.

'Hey, Dad!'

'What's up, mate?' came the call.

'I've made Mum faint again!'

'I'm coming.' He made his way out to the backyard. He stood over his wife, shook his head towards Beanz as he grinned, and then knelt to awaken her. 'What'd ya do to her this time?'

'That.' Beanz pointed to the axe head hanging out his foot. 'I think I might need to go to the hospital, Pop.'

'Oooooh. Holy shit, son. Ya think? Ya know ya nearly cut ya bloody foot off there? Ya right, mate? Did ya see what you done did to yaself?'

Holding both hands around his shin to stem the pain Beanz replied, 'Yeah. I saw it happen. It fell off the bench and I tried to catch it.'

His dad teased. 'With ya foot? Does it hurt? It looks like it hurts like hell. Phew, it hurts I reckon. I bet it hurts. It's hurtin' heaps, eh? Is it hurtin', son?'

Beanz laughed in pain with his dad. 'Yes it hurts, ya cheeky old bugger! Stop bloody reminding me.' Although Beanz was hurting they both chuckled.

Beanz's mum came back round. 'It's all right, love, you're right. Ya just fainted again's all. I'll take ya mother inside. You go hop in the car. I'll be back directly. Ha ha! You hop in the car! Fuck, I'm pretty bloody funny in a crisis, eh son?'

Beanz's dazed mother asked and teased, 'Why would ya do that? To your own bloody mother, no less. You boys, ya got nothin' bloody better ta do than make an old, brittle woman pass out.'

'Baby,' her husband assured and calmed her, 'it's nothing personal, love. It's just, you know, always been far too easy, hon. And it is, after all, so bloody funny.' She grinned as he helped her up. He told her sweetly, 'Hey. Ya not that old, love.' He smiled at her as they made their way inside arm in arm.

'Cheeky bloody bugger didn't let on. Just stood there, bleeding a bucket of blood.' Groggy, she dry retched halfway up the stairs when she recalled the fresh pool of claret. She called out and reminded Beanz, 'Cheeky bugger! Won't be so bloody funny when they cut ya bloody foot off will it? No! Or when ya catch, gang-bloody-green, then have ta chop ya leg off. No! And when ya have ta hop around every bloody where. You reckon that'll be fun? No! No, it won't! What'd ya reckon they'll all ask ya? At the hospital. Why did ya do that? You'll say, ah, you know, to make me mum faint so me and me dad could have a good old laugh at her expense. It's piss funny to watch her pass out.' She made the boys laugh and she lied, teasing, 'I heard yesterday that they've run out of anaesthetics at the hospital! So stick that up ya bum! I hope it's all bloody worth it, son.'

'It so was. Love ya, Mum!'

'Love you, pet. I'll come down to the hospital directly to see ya. Okay?'

It took some force for the nurses to remove the bright-red bloody lump of newly sharpened steel from his foot. Beanz heard, inside his head, the blade squawk and squeak against his bones when the hospital staff removed the weighty lump from its new, tight lodgings.

It had been a lengthy recovery, both boring and painful. His weeping, healing axe wound was not pretty to look at. It was easily disturbed and just as easily injured. A million dressings and three surgeries later it still wasn't right. The specialist told him he would have long-term damage, and his gait would be severely compromised.

Luce would drop around nearly every other day to check up on him. Beanz's parents liked him, and often jokes at Beanz's expense were thrown Luce's way. Beanz felt like the pain wasn't as unbearable when he visited and could have sworn on the days Luce didn't visit the wound hurt more. The pills I'm taking must be making me stupid, Beanz thought.

How was Beanz to know he was the acquaintance of the most famous of fallen angels?

Beanz noticed on his visits that Luce didn't have the scent of a man from an office, as his admitted profession might prompt him to think. He didn't smell bad, just different. The scent was thick with old engine oil, Dencorub, two-stroke exhaust and degreaser. Some of Beanz's favourite smells. A purposeful smell, albeit contradictory, as there was never one grease stain or any tell-tale dirty hands. Beanz pissed himself laughing at hearing Luce get mad about something or other when his older English accent would rise to the surface. 'Thoust this, whence that, and twain the other.'

Beanz had never been more than one hundred kilometres away from where he was born and often imagined the countries Luce came from and all those strange-talking people he grew up with. Beanz admired his intelligence. Luce was able to drop his weird accent in no time and speak like a local.

Luce was now Aussie. Aussie as free dead horse for your dog's eye.

Of course, Beanz kind of noticed the way the world followed Luce around. Almost keeping a cautious eye on him. That was the only way of phrasing in his mind what he couldn't explain other than the earth itself was bristling at Luce's presence, as if he didn't belong.

How does one explain the unexplainable?

A thought that stuck in his mind was how old Luce sounded at times. It reminded Beanz of his great-grandfather in little ways. The way they both reminisced and searched their memories perhaps, or spoke of a different time. Beanz's great-grandfather lived till he was one hundred and five. The two spoke at length about his life during Beanz's childhood. He was an intriguing man, rough, tough and a complete gentleman. He died recently. Memories of Luce witnessing a toaster do its thing, medicine at work or CPR—that stuff truly amazed him. You'd think he had never seen a pill or heard of antibiotics. All things medical were a mystery to Luce. He would tell Beanz, 'Much more efficient than hacking limbs off, or a bloodletting and leaches.' Then he would tell Beanz some sickly, medieval-sounding treatment for a common ailment, once suggesting that maggots would fix that axe wound up in no time.

Beanz was grateful for his friend's company and was glad he went fishing that day they met again. That day, when Beanz let Luce into his old green Cortina to drive him home was akin to watching man walking on the moon for the first time. He didn't seem to know about seatbelts, or car stereos. Some Motley Crue burst into life mid song from the tape deck, way too loud. Luce thought his beloved hell hounds were feasting on screaming tortured souls in the back of the car for a split second. Beanz turned the stereo down a little as they sped off, and Luce's fingers had nearly grown claws and pierced through the dashboard by the time they got into top gear. Though they were only doing eighty or so, Luce yelled in terror, 'HELLS BELLS!' And then begged Beanz to 'steady this unhinged beast and bring the savage brute to ground!'

'What do you drive back home, Luce?' Beanz asked, a little surprised.

'I didn't drive, I rode. Horses, my old Beanz, horses. This is a cursed monster! I have never travelled at such a pace.'

Beanz was laughing. 'Unhinged beast. That's piss funny, bull. I thought you were going to shit yourself then, Luce.'

'One does, just now, have the sudden urge to snap off a log.'

'I got something to show you, Luce, and I bet you shits yourself for reals this time.'

That day when they got to Beanz's place, Beanz took him to his shed out back of the house and revealed his old man's road bike.

'What is it?' Luce was besotted and a little cautious.

'It's my dad's Triumph, bull. He's away.'

No response came. But Luce, confused, stroked the bike like a horse.

'You know, a bike you can take for a run on the road. She goes like shit off a shovel.'

'But this bike, Beanz, it has no legs to run. Is she female? I can see no sign of its sex.'

'You'll see, bull.' Beanz handed him a helmet and climbed on. He then motioned Luce to do the same. He threw a leg over, jumping onto its back.

'A two-wheeled buggy, is it?'

Beanz couldn't hear Luce over the motor screaming when they accelerated off. After a while he could feel his passenger was relaxing and not crushing the life out of him as he clung on. Then he could hear

Luce plain as day, laughing and yelling with untamed joy.

Beanz yelled. 'Hold on, Luce!'

Luce didn't hear him under his helmet. Beanz opened the throttle and touched the clutch, getting the rear wheel onto its balancing point, wheel standing, scaring the bejesus out of Luce. Luce's shins were now, predictably, under Beanz's armpits as he saved himself from falling off the back of the Trumpy.

Beanz smiled like a lawyer at lunch.

MONTH FOUR

The boys surveyed the horizon while sipping their rums.

They were sitting on the verandah, watching thick gathering storm clouds bustle past a full moon.

'Bloody hell! That was close.' Beanz got a fright.

A single dog leg, smoke-stack lightning strike flashed and struck, earthing out less than forty feet away from them. The thunder clap that came with it was instantaneous and tremendous. The lads flinched at both the bright, flashing arc and the startling whip crack that was so loud it shook the wooden house and rattled their shirts like a gust from a fallen giant hardwood. The hairs on both their arms stood on end.

The power went out, though the sky's light show kept everything well lit.

Luce's savage dog fired up and complained to a flashing night sky, and then hid, shaking under the table between his master's feet like one of those dime-operated American motel massage beds.

Luce had recently adopted an abandoned wild street dog. It was a vicious, needle-toothed bastard that loved to bite. Fierce and bold as an ill-tempered cyclone, he simply hated young kids. He was ill-bred. Big eared. Filthy, tattered and abused. Evil, fearless and dangerously underfed.

He was all sinew and raw beating heart, weighing in at a mighty three kilos.

'Rex.'

The runt of his Jack Russell-Chihuahua cross litter.

The dog was instantly attracted to Luce as they crossed paths when Luce walked home from the shops with some fresh bacon in a plastic bag. Luce saw the starving animal drool at the scent of pork and his heart melted. He threw the dog a slice of bacon that was longer and wider than the animal. It didn't hit the ground long enough to get dirt on it. The mutt inhaled another four slices in that sitting alone. Another large street dog, a mean bull Arab, noticed and tried to get in on the action. That little pocket rocket revealed the size of its resolve when Rexxie pinned his ears back. Later, when Luce discovered cartoons, Rex reminded Luce of Warner Brother's 'Tasmanian Devil' but with oversized, kooky ears.

Rex followed Luce home and jumped straight onto Luce's lap when he sat on his lounge. Then Rex fell fast asleep. When Luce tried to move him, he growled and flashed pointed teeth. Then complained, exhausted, with half-hearted snarly, sleepy moans when Luce had to shift. His hounds of hell were better mannered. He imagined this fearless little creature eating from their bowls and stealing their treats.

After a few days dog and owner had reached a mutual understanding. Rex was the indisputable boss!

But a loving, loyal one. Luce felt the little bugger warming his heart. He adored Rex within a week.

After a while Michael lobbed up, out of the blue. Rex was sleeping on Luce's lap and went totally ballistic, as if he saw a hungry dingo, freaking out at the sudden, startling arrival by arcing up, barking loudly and grabbing hold of the archangel's right wing low down and growling like an angry bear cub. Heavenly feathers filled his mouth and flew, settling gently like those from a split pillow. Michael harmlessly shook his wing and flicked Rex off. As soon as his feet hit the ground he attacked again. Running this time and leaping, Rexxie grabbed the other wing for another taste, a bit higher up.

Rex instantly hated Michael. And Luce now truly loved little Rexxie.

Rex could lose the plot now and then, a benumbing habit from his past. A rat hiding could brace his focus for three days. Nothing else mattered to Rex, and Luce understood incomparable obsession. Luce took Rex swimming, and the dog had never been so pinkly tickled. Rex swam nonstop, chasing splashes off his front paws for hours. Luce would always have to go in and rescue a reluctant-to-leave, selectively deaf, unceasing, half-drowned, midget water rat as he didn't know when to stop. Luce often reminded Rex that his ancestors were bred by a priest. A priest who wanted vermin eradicated from his church. This particular priest needed a specific, enraptured, fascinating animal to ratify his situation. A courageous, intrepid beast. Athletic and capable of bedlam. What he needed was a wolverine cub to fit in all those tiny, tight rat hides. A domesticated wolverine cub. He set to work creating a talented, dexterous ratting machine, seeking out the enchanting, enamouring traits that still gift a lot of modern-day lap dogs.

The priest's name?

Jack Russell.

Luce recognised Rexxie's cleverness, how intelligent and sharp his little mind was. After meeting Michael, Rex started to dislike birds. He chased them at any opportunity, unable to get close to the many pigeons and plovers who dispersed on mass from the Esplanade. Rex recognised Beanz as a friend and soon the two were mates. Rex would smile and snarl at the same time when Beanz gave him a pat. It took a few weeks for Rex's true smile to surface without the snarly lips and for his spirit to rebuild. But when it did, it healed better than ever. Luce took him for a walk along the Esplanade each day, stopping so Rex could have a cheeky swim in the public pool. Luce never needed a leash as Rex was always on his heel and proud to be with his owner. Girls, both locals and tourists, would stop and ooh and aah over the tiny one, but Rex never let anybody but Beanz or Luce touch him. Rex was constantly keeping one eager eye open to the sky for Michael. Dreaming that big bronzed swan that suddenly appeared would one day be his.

'Wanna go to the pub?' Beanz asked.

'All right.'

The boys grabbed their usual table with a few stools around it beside a pub window. The pub was pretty empty except for a few faces hidden under their hats. Scary Mary was there, talking to some shady-looking bloke.

'Hey, Beanz, did you hear Scary Mary got busted with five pounds of sour crack?'

Scary Mary was a local prostitute whom everybody knew. She was dog-shit ugly and smelt like she looked. She was a regular at the small pub, in constant need of one bar stool for each butt cheek. Beanz nearly spat his drink out when he took a sip and laughed at Luce's joke. Her arse had more corrugations on it than the dirt road to the tip of Queensland. Then Luce said to Beanz, 'Last week some old bastard told her a joke and she laughed so hard she shit herself right where she's sitting now.'

'Dirty cow!'

'She stunk the joint out pretty good. Didn't even go to the dunny. Just smeared it all in those inflated arse cheeks of hers till quitting time. Looked like a deformed, rotten potato was hanging out of her arse crack. You could see its eyes!'

'What the fuck? She's a filthy slut! What was the joke?'

'I dunno. I couldn't hear it. Must have been a beauty though to make someone shit 'emself.'

Suddenly Mary cracked up laughing and the boys grinned, nodding at one another, wondering if she had just shat out another rotten spud.

'I bet it's bloody humid tomorrow, Luce, after all this rain.'

'Yeah it'll be a warm one. But not as humid as that drop of sweat running down Mary's un-air-conditioned arse crack around lunch time tomorrow.'

The thought was horribly green. Both chuckled to themselves. Rex was lying under the table on the cool floor with legs splayed out in front and behind him. Beanz had never seen the clouds turn on the fireworks quite like tonight. The sky was an angry stepmother. The lightning never seemed to rest. A diesel generator, keeping the pub running, purred and hummed purposely behind the rolling thunder. Neither Rex nor the boys noticed a wet, startled, savage, runaway local pig dog enter the pub. The Exchange Hotel. The Exchange was like faraway embers to men. They had to get closer to her. She was like that lonely fire on a cold black night calling to them with promises of comfort and drink. The Exchange's bar was a renowned freshly drawn bloodbath. Beanz once told Luce, 'If you're the fighting kind, or the type of person who likes to find trouble, you'll happily fill your boots in the Exchange, bull. If you have a particular malevolence, disposition, or even one of those faces, there is a plethora of blokes that will stay up all night with you just to punch the piss out of it and spit in your eye.' The French poet and novelist, Remy de Gourmont, once famously said, 'Demons are like obedient dogs: they come when called.' The Exchange Hotel was many a man's obedient dog. Last year Beanz, pissed and cock-eyed, climbed onto the pub's roof and spray painted a big, fat, red S in front of its sign for the whole suburb to see. Got himself banned for a few weeks from The SExchange Hotel.

The big fella skulked towards Rexxie, approaching Rex from behind. When he was close a breeze gave him away, and Rex sprang into action, scaring the shit out of the boys when the two dogs burst into life under their table. Rexxie grabbed the brindle bull Arab on the snout. It shook Rex loose and chased after the little one on the tiled pub floor. Rex stepped sideways when the bull Arab charged after gaining some footing. As the runaway slid past a side-stepping Rex with the anchors on full, Rexxie grabbed him by the nuts. The big dog was still sliding, yelping, trying desperately to sit on Rex and get him away from his 'nads. Rex got out from behind him before being sat on and, leaping, attacked his snout again, making the big dog stand on all fours again as he stopped sliding. Rex let go of its nose and raced around behind him to again bite its aggots. The bull Arab got his balls ripped every time he stood and his nose bitten every time he sat. Up and down. Up and down it went till Luce plucked Rex off the ground. Rex was well pissed, struggling, writhing and wriggling to break free. Luce couldn't hold him as he slipped back to the ground. The meddlesome bull Arab was waiting and caught Rexxie midair, before he even hit the deck, catching him by a front leg and shoulder. Rexxie screamed as incisors pierced his flesh and then clamped down, breaking bone. He was violently flung into a wall before Luce could again save his furry little friend. Rexxie was in shock and fell back to his default self, growling and snarling. His right front leg hung torn from his shoulder and blood drenched him red. He was opened up good. Beanz kicked the frenzied bull Arab in the guts. 'Fuck off, ya bastard!'

As it yelped and ran off, Rex barked, 'Fuck off, ya bastard!' at the bully also. They raced to Beanz's car to get to the vet. Luce said, 'Let's go to the hospital!'

Beanz told him they couldn't. 'We gotta get him to the vet, Luce, before he bleeds out.'

'What is the vet?'

'An animal hospital, Luce. Haven't you ever needed a vet for your horses?'

'I'm afraid that if this happened to a horse we would need a rifle, not one of these vets. Can vets help him?'

Rex was screaming, thrashing blood in pain onto Luce's lap.

Luce focused on his dog and shifted some of Rex's pain. His powers were very weak so he concentrated. Rexxie's screaming settled to loud moans. The vet was closed so, in pet emergencies, the small suburb went to the vet's own home. He stabilised Rex there and gave him blood straightaway. Then stitched him up with many little drains installed. The leg wasn't broken and that stumped the vet. 'I can see on the X-ray where it has been snapped, but then healed over. Has Rex had a broken leg before?' Luce admitted Rexxie was a stray and that he didn't know. 'Very strange.'

Beanz sat outside on the vet's verandah and smiled when he saw Rex in Luce's arms, out of it on pain killers, but alive. Luce got home, and when Beanz left he heard Rex growl groggily at Michael.

'You're willing to end your time here for this dog?'

Luce didn't answer. Michael kneeled beside little Rexxie on his blanket.

'You would use your power to help Rexxie?'

Rex growled long and slow. Still no answer. Luce knew this couldn't be good. Now and then his holidays were cut short for unacceptable bad behaviour.

'You love, Rex?'

'Yes.'

'Do you think Rex knows what you are?'

Rex tried to bark at hearing his name twice spoken by the ugly golden swan. Yes, ugly golden swan. The vet's drugs, they were working just fine.

'He knows what I am.'

'What of Beanz?'

'He is my friend.'

'Oh. The king needs company?'

'No.'

'Are you his friend, dear enemy.'

'Yes.'

'So you would weep for him?'

'Yes. He is a good man.'

'He is a child.'

'True. Though I'm sure you're not the first to underestimate him. He's an old soul who makes wise decisions.'

Michael got to the point. 'The Old Man is upset. You should never have healed Rex's leg.'

'I have no powers to do such a thing,' he lied.

'There are still traces. That's why we installed Commandment One.'

'What of my fate, Michael?'

Michael was gone, and Luce still here. If it was expulsion he would not be on earth.

He lifted Rex from the blanket nest on the ground to his bed and lay with him, stroking under his chin. 'You showed that big mongrel, didn't ya? You're so big and terribly brave, Rexxie. So, so strong aintcha mate? He was a giant that fulla!' Rexxie pushed his head groggily into Luce's hand. 'I thought I was going to lose you, little mate.'

The two slept. The traces Michael spoke of helped Rex heal fast. Also, that night helped Beanz's foot to come good in record time. Turns out the Old Man thought Lucifer couldn't be held responsible for residual power out of his control, so fair warning was issued. Michael reported to the Big Fella and God noticed that Michael was perplexed.

'What has you troubled?'

'I think he is feeling love again.'

His boss smiled.

MONTH FIVE

Luce had enjoyed and listened to music on many of his previous visits.

He found music very acceptable now and then. From flute players to sitars and drums of both war and peace. He had heard Mozart, in fact all the classical greats. Luce had always been moved and stupefied at their glorious sounds. He had listened to plenty of gospel music over the ages. On this visit he discovered rock and roll.

He heard first a little Motley Crue that day fishing with Beanz, but his ears hadn't been prepared for that sudden blast of noise. When Beanz first play Hendrix on the car stereo, Luce had to ask how many musicians it took to play that mighty sound. When Beanz said three, Luce couldn't really grasp the concept of modern bands and it took time to get his head around electrified music, modern drummers and amplified guitars. Beanz notice how Luce's ears picked up on tasty music, so he introduced him to all the bands he loved. Beanz's dad had a wide and eclectic taste in music so Beanz knew the greats well. Beanz suggested to Luce that he should watch Rage on TV and see the bands in action. Luce did, and many a Saturday night he would stay up with the moon and watch the Rage specials. Luce decided that John Henry Bonham was the duck's nuts and fucking brilliant, and bought a drum kit and cymbals of the same dimensions and brand as John Henry's. He had only watched drummers on TV, and Luce playing his shiny new Ludwig kit sounded like a drunken octopus happily thrashing away, or skeletons rave dancing on an iron roof. Beanz told him he needed lessons and teased, 'You sound like a plumber, not a drummer!'

Luce found a drum teacher and, once a week, he attended lessons. The drum teacher was in his early forties, cool and laid back. He'd had an accident ten years beforehand and these days he couldn't rotate and move around the kit as he once did, but he still had some fat chops. He was a patient teacher who made playing drums uncomplicated. Luce practised each day for a couple of hours through the middle of the day to keep the peace with his neighbours and had been playing for two months. Luce was no more talented than the next man, but practised and could play four-bar grooves with a small selection of basic fills. He loved syncopation and the challenge of the independence of limbs. Soon the drunken octopus was sobered and gaining coordination. He could hold a basic rhythm together at this point and roll around the kit in time. He started to hear the music on the page as opposed to seeing notes. Beanz could hear the improvement and found his foot tapping along with one or two beats Luce practised here and there. Luce decided he would have a suitable drum kit waiting for him at home. Hell could do with some rock and roll, he thought.

One day Beanz played 'Highway to Hell', performed by AC/DC, as they drove around town. Not in all Luce's years had he heard anything like Bon Scott and the boys. His grin was as wide as the windscreen when he heard Bon's ode to hell.

'Can we play that again?' he asked excitedly. Acca Dacca fever gripped Luce, and he was their staunchest, fiercest fan. He bought every album AC/DC recorded and cranked them up loud, playing his drum kit along with Phil Rudd. He tried to copy and emulate every note and groove, giving the kit a good spanking. Even Luce had to admit that his face bore a cheeky resemblance to the mighty Bon when he first clamped eyes on the legend himself singing 'Jail Break'. Shirts with Angus or Bon on the front and albums fast appeared as his fever held. He didn't want to join a band. He just liked to play in his house with his rock gods on the stereo. He could see Jimmy Page hypnotising the crowd, see Bon grinning like a melon thief. Imagined Jimmy Hendrix burning his fender as they jammed together. Music was immortality. Until this visit he had never heard of rock and roll, so when movies on TV said rock and roll music was the devil's music, he said out loud, 'I didn't have bloody nothing to do with it!' He copped it for the blues as well. He wasn't even in the Americas, and had never been to any famous crossroad to meet a musician, ever. Still they blamed him.

Luce was fortunate enough to be present in Europe during the golden years of classic art. He saw firsthand the grandeur of the rising architecture, statues and talent those years produced. Today's art intrigued him. From album covers to jewellery, he was in awe. Tattoos were on nearly every other person, with all sorts of individual tastes and modern styles on display. He loved watching the buzz saw paint through the tattooist's windows. He decided he would get one as soon as he came up with a suitable idea.

He had found Bob Marley recently and played his albums more and more. When he tried to jam with the Wailers on his stereo he didn't know where to start. The reggae rhythm sounded backwards or disjointed to his ears and he just stared at the drumsticks in his hands, not having a clue what to do with them. Luce decided that Bob's was music he would listen to and not jam to. It would take time to learn and absorb those broken backward beats.

Luce was keen to go for a road trip and explore some new places for a few weeks and asked if Beanz would drive, if Luce shouted the fuel, food and accommodation. Beanz agreed after thinking about it for a moment. And Broome was their chosen destination. Beanz figured, within that long moment, that Luce would be an excellent bloke to travel and experience new places with. Sharing a road trip, even footy trips on a bus for a couple of days with his footy mates, could get old and scruffy pretty fast. Beanz could foresee none of those issues with Luce. His house was always tidy, and Beanz never once heard the 'plop and slop' of raw dog food smattering Luce's dining-room floor when feeding Rexxie. Rexxie had his own bowls and did not eat off Luce's plates at the table. Beanz decided that sharing his car and travelling with Luce and Rexxie would be relatively clean, laid back and unobtrusive.

They drove across the red raw top end with an eager Jack Russell's head out either one of the back widows. With some smart purchases they took their time and relaxed, camping in a new tent with an Esky full of food, dog chow and alcohol. Luce loved the wide spaces and that huge, cloudless sky. He adored the heat that proved even warmer than Cairns, and how the bitumen looked sunburnt. The wildlife caught his attention. Everything seemed larger out there. The lizards and wedge-tailed eagles were monolithic. The blow flies were thick and the size of pigeons. There was plenty of 'Poison Rope' wriggling onto the tin-roof-hot bitumen, baking in the ever-present sunshine. The spiders' bodies were larger than his hand. The roos, the giant reds, captured perfectly the roaming, enduring wild spirit of Australia. Rexxie sniffed something interesting. He investigated and found a big old lace-tail monitor lizard resting in the shade of a small shrub. He was about to claim it as his, by cocking a leg and pissing on it. Rexxie yelped when the strange-looking, weird-smelling stick burst into hissing life, and like an angry dinosaur chased the little bloke off. Rex shat himself while back tracking, wide eyed, a million miles an hour, screaming like a dropped baby as he turned heel and legged it back to the safety of Luce and Beanz.

Cable Beach and its beautiful clean sands were a welcome sight, and both human and canine leapt out of the thick, dusty red Cortina that was actually green underneath those caked on layers, into the turquoise

Indian Ocean to wash the unrelenting heat and pindan off. They camped in a dog-friendly caravan park close to beach and bar, setting up their tent amongst a host of other travellers and tourists. A couple of German girls on holiday needed help to set their tent up and Luce and Beanz gave them a hand. Cavita, one of the girls— she was the most talkative, lean, tall and dark eyed— flirted with Luce, calling him handsome in a rugged type of way. They saw a fair bit of each other over the next few days. Beanz almost didn't recognise Luce when he spoke perfect German to the girls. Beanz told him later at the bar, 'Shit, man, I had my back to you. I thought their angry-sounding German boyfriends had shown up! Where did you learn to speak German so well?'

'Why, Germany, Beanz.'

'You lived in Germany?'

'Once. I have lived almost everywhere due to my work.'

'And you say you hate your job.'

'I do.'

'But you get to see the world, Luce. You can't beat that.'

'I see nothing but numbers. My time off is the only time I see anything.'

'So how often do you get time off?'

Luce inhaled deeply and sighed. 'Not nearly often enough, my friend.'

'What, like every year?'

'Feels more like a hundred.'

'I hear ya, mate.'

'Everything changes so much each time I get a break. People change and places change.'

'You work too hard, Luce. Yeah, you got all this money, but how much living do you miss while earning it?'

'You're right. And I have recently petitioned for two breaks in the time I usually have one.'

'Me old man says far too many young people die from old age. So I reckon that's a good start, mate. What did they say?'

'My father hasn't replied as of now. But I think I have earned it.'

'Fuck yeah, you've earned it! Two breaks a year won't kill anyone.'

'If only that year didn't feel like a century.'

'Work always makes time pass slow, Luce. But shit, man, I reckon even the Devil himself must get a couple of days off now and then.'

'What did you say?'

'You know? Even Lucifer must go on leave.'

Lucifer on leave, eh? Luce thought to himself. Truer words have never been spoken, my old Beanz.

Beanz was happy in Broome.

He had never observed the sun setting over the ocean before and every evening the boys would take Rex, a joint and a couple of drinks to watch the girls and camels walk the beach as the sun kissed Broome goodbye. The iron oxide dust and pindan floating, suspended briefly in the atmosphere, gave the three boys the best sunsets they had ever seen. The beach seemed to go on forever, the sands whiter and cleaner than anything at home.

They dined now and then at a fine restaurant tucked away in the five-star resort on the beach.

The boys took the German girls barra fishing and crabbing and caught some beauties to keep, clean and eat back at the campsite.

Luce relaxed deeply. There was nowhere to be and no schedule. The town itself was clean, sleepy, dreamy and in no hurry, leaving no place they'd rather be. Afternoon beers, fresh seafood, tasty joints, stunning sunsets, good company, sweet night-time temperatures and endless blue skies made it the best time Luce had ever had on earth.

Luce decided, These Australian's sure know how to live life.

The boys were four shades browner after the first week. For Beanz, Broome was a perfect change from Cairns and the east coast. The red, thirsty earth was a complete contrast to the emerald forest of home. And the beaches were so long that he couldn't see their end. People could drive their four-wheel drives on the nude beach, tide depending, to gain access to endless places to visit.

Beanz tried to help with the costs but Luce would have none of it. 'Save your money for your education, my friend,' was his go-to response. Beanz really didn't have much money for anything. His family wasn't well off. Luce knew this and never let Beanz feel uncomfortable about money. 'It's my treat. After all, it's your car and you do all the driving, my old Beanz.' So Beanz relaxed and soon came to grips with his mate's generosity. 'What use is money if it isn't to spend, Beanz?'

And spend he did. The church in Cairns had a large cardboard box full of cash. Many, many Sunday donations waited for him. Luce's holiday pay. Luce upgraded their lodgings to the resort for a week of absolute luxury and they made the most of all the facilities, even with Rex, at a five-star cost, of course. Beanz felt a little fat and bloated from all the room service, so after a walk on the beach he wondered around the resort grounds, stumbling across a health club the resort provided. His foot had been bothering him and hurting from lack of movement and all the sitting/driving demanded of him. Beanz was expecting a smelly old gym, vain bodybuilders and rusty gear but was surprised to find the building was clean, didn't stink, had a verandah, and inside had an impressive, sumptuous wooden floor with modern gear. The bloke who ran the gym was an ex-boxer who did lots of one-on-one work with people who liked to box for fitness. He had a great existence there and his well-liked, well-mannered white dog, stained red from pindan, was always on the verandah, in front of a slightly ajar door keeping his ten-year-old body cool in the escaping air-conditioned air. Surprisingly, old Buddy and young Rexxie got on great. The gym smelt good, clean and matched the five-star standard of the resort it supported. Beanz could maintain the rehab work for his foot that his physio and doctor prescribed. Lots of locals worked out there, and, being such a friendly place, people said g'day to each other and inquired about your day and invited the two boys along to local get-togethers. Luce tagged along to have a look the second time Beanz went and the boys got on well with the bloke who ran the gym. They all went to a bar and joked, drank, smoked, laughed and talked shit all night. During the last week they had become quite social within the township and made the most of what Broome's pristine coastline offered.

They were both sad to leave North Western Australia.

When they returned to Cairns, Beanz decided the Pacific's salt water would help his wound heal. He drove to the northern beaches most days for a walk and some swimming, inviting Rexxie and Luce along. Soon, some beach fishing gear would accompany them, and then Beanz's old man's tinny and spearguns. Luce was in awe of the bommies and coral stands that they snorkelled. He had never spearfished in any ocean and had never really seen underwater sea activities before, not like those the Coral Sea or Great Barrier Reef offered.

The reef was sensationally other worldly. Her confronting, befooling elegance enchanted Luce's human condition. Before diving, Beanz gave Luce some worldly, solid, local, swimming-the-reef advice, while slipping on their fins and goggles.

'Dead set, Luce. If ya don't know what it is, don't touch it! And if ya do know what it is, don't touch it!'

Beanz mentioned cone shells and the danger that came with picking them up. He also warned Luce about blue-ringed octopus, jellyfish and a few other hidden dangers the reef contained. Luce was reminded that unrivalled beauty is often evenly matched with unrivalled vices.

Vibrant colours of bright neon and schools of uncountable fish, both in numbers and varieties, were matched only in size by Luce's sentiment, smiles and whoops of underwater laughter. Sea turtles, calm as a gathering of priests, drifted casually by him, and friendly dugongs were a hypnotist's watch to Luce's eager, hungry eyes. The silence of this strange watery empire was unearthly. The blue underwater horizon endless on clear, still days.

Luce wished he could hold his breath longer. Up and down the depths the boys dived, swam and hunted, gaining new breath to find a good-sized, tasty coral fish. Luce watched Beanz point the spear gun and fire at his quarry. A snap of underwater sound and a diluted cloud of blood exploded from behind the head of a fat red emperor. It leapt in fright, swimming erratically, fighting the spear and rope when Beanz pull him in and fetched the trophy fish to the anchored tinny. Luce then circled a lion's mane coral collection and investigated the many busy creatures that called it home. Fascinated, he surfaced and regained a fresh lung full. He dove to the ten-metre-deep sandy bottom and witnessed the many shrimps, snails, starfish, and sand-dwelling creatures of all shapes, colours and description that were almost impossible to explain. Fast-moving fish, slow, docile fish, industrious fish, fat fish, skinny fish, coral fish, ribbon fish, sand fish. So many sorts of fish!

Luce fell heavily. It was love at first sight. An unbreakable love. The reef was Luce's kryptonite. He was powerless within its glory. Its stunning perfection muted him. Its breathtaking beauty amazed him.

Beanz was also hunting for some crayfish on this particular trip. The reef was spectacular at this location, and Beanz told him the changes in water depth and temperature at this spot created a huge variety of corals and life.

Clear, healthy, practically invisible water surrounded them. So clear that when Luce looked back to the tinny from a distance it appeared to be floating on air. Some corals were plate shaped, some mushroom and cactus like. Others looked like large, leafless trees, spray painted with bright fluorescent colours. A few looked alien. Many corals here at this reef were fine and delicate, like translucent angel's-hair pasta or jellyfish tentacles, their many strands drifting here and there like a mermaid's long hair. If Luce closed his eyes down there and concentrated he could hear the buzzing and swooshing of marine wildlife amongst the colourful array and tangle of sea forest. That was when an eel hiding in among some deeper rocks caught Luce's attention. He resurfaced and cleaned some fog out of his goggles and then swam in the eel's direction, duck diving to the rocky outcrop to have a close look at him. On the way down he paused when a mighty stingray came into sight. The grace with which it moved reminded Luce of a large linen sheet hanging on a clothes line, drying, curling and rippling along its length to a gentle breeze. He watched the ray for so long that he needed another breath. On his return dive he visited the eel, snaking, twisting and curling into its new abode.

It was all too beautiful as Luce floated like a starfish on his back looking up into the cloudless blue sky. 'One more dive,' Luce whispered to himself as he made his way back to the tinny. This time when he dived under there were no fish.

Not a single one.

As he made his way towards the bottom he noticed how lifeless and empty the many corals were. Where did everything go? The clusters of coral garden among which he held his breath were empty and deserted. A few metres from the bottom he hovered for a closer squiz within the coral, looking for signs of life. The reef suddenly felt like a dark, haunted, shadowed jungle when all other life forms had exited. When he turned to ascend, he turned to a butt-clenching surprise. There was a face in front of his. A large, ugly face. The proprietor of a sinister smile. A mean, toothsome, unfriendly smile. An air bubble escaped Luce's mouth in shock. The grin he was faced with was heavy and deadly serious. Muscular, bulky shoulders behind the grin were larger and much broader than its head.

They both were still as the reef's current gently pushed them away from the coral stand into the clear, open water. Luce felt nervous. The five-metre tiger shark's snout almost touched his own. He couldn't control his fears and more oxygen escaped his lungs when he mournfully cried out. The tiger shark rudely forced and stuffed its nuzzle under Luce's armpit, aggressively pushing Luce's frozen-stiff body over to the horizontal. Rag-dolled, Luce was frozen. He quickly surmised his skin and bones were no match for that rack of rowed buzz saws. Luce felt his heart beating in his ears as the shark pushed and shoved him around like a dog with a beach ball. Luce didn't know what to do. He certainly wasn't going to touch or punch it! The current swirling around the corals moved Luce further away from the coral's perceived safety. So, Luce stayed deadly still. The shark investigated like a burly bear sniffing a sack of raw meat. He manoeuvred Luce with boisterous, tempestuous bursts of violence. Luce's lung full of air was fast running out and starting to burn hot inside him. Luce had been man/shark handled back into a vertical position. The shark used his granite head, rudely probing and carelessly prodding Luce's body, feeling strange textures, smelling fear and its familiarities. The tiger shark was now face to face with Luce and stared unblinkingly, piercing into Luce, searching with cold, severe, black-as-death eyes of sin. Luce supposed that all things stopped. He was heavily outweighed, and completely out of his element. Time, the earth, the fishes, the corals, his heart, his out-of-control twitching sphincters even paused. A perfectly human response. The only muscles that locked in for him were those of his face. It was a contorted, sour, almost scribed-in-stone look. A frozen-in-fear-and-carbon Han Solo moment. Hovering like a half-sunk battleship mid depth, they drifted. Luce felt instantly insignificant and completely vulnerable. His fear and adrenalin chemical cocktail levels were off the charts as his whole body was now burning heart-rendering hot from lack of fresh air.

Thus ends my dreams. Fuck! This is gunna hurt. God's gunna have me eaten.

The tiger shark beat his tail assertively, and the small gap between them closed fast. Luce covered his face and closed his eyes so he couldn't see. In total panic and chaos he tried to remember quickly all the smells, the tastes, the friends, the ocean, the fun, music and feelings this visit to earth offered. Luce was powerless. OH SHIT. I don't wanna go yet! The shark sped menacingly at him. Its face and eyes were severe, uncourteous and revealed no recognisable emotion or read. Disdainfully, the tiger shark swung his solid head and jarred Luce out of its way, making sure his goliath-like, five-metre-long, sandpaper, rough-hewn body violently struck Luce's as it left. Luce watched the pendulous tail of this prosaic, slow-moving monster swim off into the deep blue. And felt the exact moment time returned.

Beanz had seen the whole thing from a distance and cluster shat for his mate. He tried firing the spear gun towards the shark as he got closer, but Luce and that gargantuan eating machine were too far away. The shark seemed to Beanz to be toying with Luce, playing, dallying with him before the kill. Pushing him around, intimidating him and getting up in his face. When the beast lunged wildly at Luce, Beanz thought it was all over red rover. Fortunately for Luce the shark had recently dined. He was full, chock-a-block, and uninterested in eating him. The troublemaker mercifully pushed Luce out of the way, letting him know in no uncertain terms, 'Ya fuckin' lucky I already ate, mate.'

It was one of the single scariest things Beanz had ever seen. 'Tiger sharks, bull. Can be a fucking handful. Specially solid, five-metre, bad-to-the-bone saws like him.' When they got back to the tinny there was no pomp but much ceremony when they told each other what they had seen and felt.

'From where I was swimming, bull,' Beanz told him, 'it looked like a mullet kissing a bus!'

In hindsight's presence they were silenced. That run in, though, didn't put Luce off the sea at all. If anything, the opposite was true. When the weather allowed it, they took the opportunity to go reef fishing and diving. The fish and food caught tasted fresh and flavoursome. Each time Luce dived under the surface he saw something new, something that stunned his mind and captured his heart, sometimes making him shake his head in disbelief or nod his head with approval. The reef was not part of this world when Luce was God's right-hand man. If it was, the old timer never told Luce about it. Even the Devil himself can appreciate earthly perfection. The Great Barrier Reef, for Luce, was female. She was a spiritually gifted, magically divine ocean forest sprite. She was an untainted Garden of Eden. Untainted by man. Luce hoped man loved her as he did. She is feminine and glorious, he thought.

MONTH SIX

Luce discovered movies when Beanz brought over his DVD player and a few films. Beanz left it at Luce's place along with a selection of some modern-day porn. Not since the ancient Romans had Luce seen the likes of Debbie Does Dallas, or Linda Lovelace in action. Sex out of wedlock was everywhere, porn, both straight and gay, in every single DVD store.

Boy/goat/sheep shagging aristocrats and priests of antiquity had less kinky sex than people nowadays, he thought. Women were revealing more and more flesh on the street, and distinguishing prostitutes from regular women out in nightclubs and drinking on the town was almost impossible. Women were sometimes men, and some men women now. The world had certainly gotten a hell of a lot sluttier. He admired this bold sexual revolution. Luce also appreciated the newest freedoms found. Women voting, indigenous peoples having rights, child slavery abolished. The death penalty was a memory, a thing of Australia's past. Christianity was still in the ether, but people no longer lived their lives according to its every word. The many frailties of man were ever rising, and more and more souls sent to Satan. Greed, avarice, vanity, gluttony, covetousness were now a celebrated, common, appealing life style and a daily part of every first-world society. The lack of man's self-control and discipline he witnessed each day confirmed that his job was only going to get busier.

Had everyone forgotten the consequences for such behaviour?

Had they forgotten the debt to be paid for these trespasses?

It was as if Sodom and Gomorra had copulated, or a part of Hades had spilled over to this world with him with each visit. Every night on the news and in the daily papers there were murders, rapes and violence. Every other week, mass-murdering sprees with unthinkable weapons of all description. The wars. How he noticed those. How they never ended.

Horses were now a hobby for mankind. In fact, the average man had never so much as patted one. Horse racing made him happy momentarily when he saw the animals running. Then saddened him that they were now nothing more than a sideshow for the wealthy and gamblers.

Trucks, semi-trailers, airplanes, motorcycles and even modern bicycles confused and intrigued him. Engines took a little figuring out. He was positive that horses were the explanation. Only when Beanz explained pistons, crankshafts and internal combustion did he shelve the horse-trapped-inside-the-engine-block idea. Electricity and running water were his pet delights. The night he arrived it was the street lights and the lit buildings that first caught his attention. Then the automobiles and their bright headlights. Not kerosene or oil street lamps of old that barely cast a shadow. Each time he turned a tap on and water magically appeared, he smiled. Not having to shit in the backyard pleased him, and that same satisfied smile appeared when he watched the toilet flush. Luce decided that using soft, three-ply toilet paper to wipe his arse with was as close to heaven as he would ever get. Much more acceptable than the leaves, bark and crude communal facilities he had explored throughout his past visits.

The bowels of hell could use a little modern lighting and plumbing, he promised himself. They hadn't been upgraded since he copied the Romans' aqueducts.

Luce found himself watching General Hospital and a lot of medicine-related shows on the TV. Man had truly come far. Leaches, bloodletting, and cruel potions were gone. Once, when Beanz looked a little down, Luce told him to fart into a jar and screw the lid on, and then unscrew and sniff it when he was feeling somewhat melancholic. Beanz cried laughing, a little worried Luce wasn't joking. Not once had Luce seen any of the doctors on General Hospital use bloodletting or make a patient fart into a jar to take home to medicate themselves with later.

The world was shrinking with the help of telephones, television and now computers. Everything happened faster today. If you wanted anything you could get it. Overnight if you were impatient. If something dramatic happened in the world you heard about it straightaway, not months or years later as was sometimes the case in the past. Each century Luce visited previously moved slowly forward, and time was needed for change. Human beings' progress recently seemed inexhaustible, their cunning and determination one-eyed and driven. When would enough be enough, he wondered? It was an age of incomparable population, but also an age of galling loneliness. Humans were growing ever older through scientific medicine and the use of good, dependable food sources. The search for energy was destroying precious farming lands. The need and greed for timber and housing were devastating the world's forests. Humans had a God-given right to breed, and population growth was already untenable for some countries. A hole the size of Antarctica was consuming their fragile ozone layer. Man had destroyed the stratosphere in one foul industrial age, leaving wealth, hunger, decadence, suffering and homelessness on a scale never before imagined or witnessed. The earth was turning on man and he was undisciplined, stubborn and too out of control to care, Luce thought.

His goddamned human emotions would empathise with those skinny, starving kids on those TV ads. Fly-blown, breathing skeletons, who could easily survive on the excess wasted food from one modern society, feeding nobody, rotting in landfills. It perplexed his rational emotions, his common sense. All this luxury on the one hand, so much pestilence in the other. Man was making a mess of everything. Even the Devil could see it. Lucifer had helped create this world we inhabit. He loved it. Much more than he loved man. He was, after all, known as the 'Bringer of Light' and, for a time, 'Son of the Dawn'. Man treated the planet like it treated all disposable goods within its reach. It was a throwaway earth. Now they were searching for and spending countless dollars on finding a new planet to ravish, bind and rape. God gave to them one home. One Eden alone. He only built one residence for man. There was no fall-back plan or earth take two. Those hundreds of billions of dollars and colossal energies could have fed and powered the planet, raising the standard of living worldwide at the same moment, a hundred times over. But foolishly man thought he knew better and had that eternal curse. That sickly disease they called hope. Hope didn't feed the masses. Hope didn't repair the damage man had done to this lonely blue speck floating within the emptiness of the lifeless heavens. Lucifer knew there was no new home for humankind. Lucifer also knew that once this one was gone, so would be the spark called life. God would have to cleanse this land if it was to heal. Something had to give. Luce knew that nature had a cure for this kind of madness. Luce found himself wondering if God gave the wrong species dominion over the rest. Wolves, Luce decided, would have been a less indulgent choice than man.

Alcohol and his drug of choice were his favourite perks in this modern age. Rum and cannabis were a daily part of his life. He had, of course, dealt with the casualties of the ancient Opium Wars. Luce had seen firsthand man chasing the dragon's tail. He had witnessed every boom mankind sparked—financial, gold, minerals—then that boom's inevitable bust. He had seen all the tragedies of antiquity.

It was during this time that he met Frankie. Frankie was in Cairns on holiday from Sydney. Frankie was Chinese and about twenty-seven. She was a smaller girl but made up for her lack of height with great legs and a pretty face. She had lived in Australia since she was eight years old and no hint of a Chinese accent remained. Her own mother called her a banana, white and Aussie on the inside, yellow and Chinese on the outside.

Luce had just eaten lunch at a cheaper, nastier Chinese restaurant and, on his short walk home, he had become violently ill. Rushing for a small, hot-boxed, red-brick public toilet on the busy Esplanade he vomited heavily as his sphincter went spastic and shot out an uncompromising hot fountain of horror. He nearly destroyed and cut the dunny's bowl clean in half with his gas-axe, high-pressure brown bum water. There was plenty of splash back. The stench was thick, humid and far too toxic for the atmosphere to readily absorb. He flushed, rested, moaned and repeated, lying for a while sprawled awkwardly on the floor, his hot, forsaken forehead resting on the cool porcelain as the stink permeated. A middle-aged American tourist walked in to have a piss and quickly decided he could wait. The American dry retched and groaned! The bloke turned heel after getting an unventilated, warm whiff of that fresh hell. When Luce walked from the toilet heading home he had to vomit a few more times. A dodgy oyster he had eaten was quick to react. He was pasty, sweating, stumbling, moaning, and vomit randomly leapt from his mouth and streamed uncontrollably from his nose. A young Asian lady with a thick Aussie accent asked if he was okay as she walked by.

'I'm crook. Dodgy oyster.' Two syllable words were triggering his guts.

'Where are you headed.'

'Home.'

Luce felt he was watching himself from afar, like an external, sickly, astral-travelling witness.

'I will help you home, mate. I'm Frankie.' She offered Luce a small, soft, firm hand.

Luce was in a real state, pale, clammy and feeling awful. 'I'm Luce.' Yep, two syllables was it. In his delirium he didn't notice pretty Frankie was, in fact, a man. Frank. A passable cross dresser.

Luce just saw a pretty, friendly Asian girl in bright pink, tiny socks and runners helping him. Brown, lean legs. Short, frayed denim pants and a sports top revealed a feminine mid-section, a belly button ring with jade on her skin. He was far too sick to pay any more heed than that. She walked with him and waited patiently, offering support as he threw up in random bushes and shrubs. By the time they got to Luce's house he had fertilised/poisoned most of the flora growing along the Esplanade. She saw him inside and to his shower, and then his bed. She found a bucket and left that on the floor beside where he lay on his bed. Frankie opened the fridge to see what she could do. She found a defrosted chicken and a few onions, vegetables and a large pot, and then started to prepare chicken soup. She noticed Rex when he investigated the fridge with her.

'Hello, little fella.'

Frankie picked up the dog and asked him what his name was.

'I will just call you Cutie for now.'

93

She found a piece of silverside in the fridge and gave it to Rexxie.

'Here ya go, Cutie. Ya hungry?'

Rex never left her side after that. She wet a face cloth and folded it, placing it on Luce's forehead. She made him sip water each time she and Rexxie came in.

Frankie loved Luce's old-fashioned wooden house. She had never stayed in a Queenslander before. The house was small with two bedrooms, lifted slightly on stumps so the Pacific's legendary breeze could find its way around the whole house. The home was comfortably composed, cool and quaint. The downstairs laundry, toilet and bathroom floor was a red-painted slab of concrete with an old-fashioned, deep, claw-foot bathtub and lots of room to swing your cat. Within an hour the house was smelling great from the soup. Luce slept after he could vomit no more. When he arose he felt much better. Not great but better. Night time and soup caught his senses, and then he noticed the spew bucket had been freshly emptied and washed. He washed his face downstairs and saw his sickly complexion. His body was starving but he was not at all hungry. He could hear Frankie watching the television, laughing along with it.

'Hello, Luce.' She was relaxed on the couch with Rex fast asleep on her lap. She got up to see him. 'I love your little home.'

'G'day, Frankie. Yeah, it's a great little house.'

'I hope you don't mind. I hung around just in case you got worse, and I made myself at home. I rolled a joint or two from your bowl.'

'Please, I don't mind. You are welcome, and thank you for helping me home. I don't think I would have made it back here on my own.' The smell of soup tempted his stomach. 'The house smells wonderful.'

'It was my pleasure. Chicken soup is always good for you when your belly's sick. What's your dog's name?'

'That little fella's name's Rex.'

'Rex has been great company and a perfect gentleman.'

Luce sat at the table, still a bit wobbly and crook. Rexxie sat worried on his master's lap and affectionately licked Luce's chin. Frankie ladled two bowls of soup.

'Mmmmm, that's so good. I wasn't hungry till I smelt this.'

'Are you feeling better, Luce?'

He placed Rexxie on the ground. 'Yes. Much better, thanks. This soup calms my guts. You have no trace of an Asian accent, Frankie,' he said between sips. She explained how that came about. She did speak some Cantonese. Luce then greeted her with a traditional Cantonese welcome and she had to admit in shock to him when she responded in the dialect that her language was that of an eight-year-old child. That was when she moved to Australia and learnt English.

'What do you do, Luce? And how come your Cantonese is so good?'

'Oh, it's a little rusty. I visited China some years ago. I'm an accountant. I'm on leave for a little while, so I set up base for a year here in Cairns.'

'I love Cairns. It's far too busy in Sydney, way too fast. Cairns is just the right pace for me.'

'What do you do in Sydney?'

'I'm a doctor, a registrar. But my family owns a restaurant.'

'A Chinese restaurant?'

'Yes.'

'That's where I got sick. From oysters. I ate them at a little place in town.'

'You wouldn't get sick from my family's cooking. We have a large successful business. My parents are very traditional and strict. So they have their fears and suspicions.'

'About what?'

'They suspect, you know …?'

'No, I don't know.'

'I'm a cross dresser.'

This was a phrase Luce had not yet heard.

'A what?'

'Can't you tell? I'm a bloke.'

Luce looked a little closer.

'Oh. Now I see.' Luce smiled. 'I didn't notice until you mentioned it.'

'Does that worry you?'

'No.' He was enjoying his soup. 'You are a friendly, cute girl that helped me. That's all I saw and need to know.'

Frankie flirted harmlessly with him. 'You're so sweet.'

'It's only right to thank and be courteous to someone who's assisted me.'

'Well I'm glad a gentleman still exists. I meet a lot of pigs when I dress up.'

'Not many people would call me a gentleman.'

'Well, you're old fashioned and kind, you're friendly and you are thankful. That's what a gentleman does.'

'So, you're a doctor within a Sydney hospital?'

'Yes, I've just finished six months rotation in the emergency department.'

'That sounds interesting.'

'Yes. Oh my god, it's so busy. The things I see, Luce. You wouldn't believe some of the things I've seen.'

'Like what?'

'Ha! Well, in six months I saw at least half a dozen blokes, old, young, married, skinny, big, all sorts, with batteries, broom sticks, even a vacuum cleaner and glass bong pipes wedged up their arses. One reckoned he fell over onto a broom handle and when it wouldn't come out he snapped it off in there.'

Luce burst out laughing.

'Lots of Sydney's men fall onto things. I once had a cheeky long-term head-injury patient on the ward who dressed up in a doctor's outfit with a stethoscope around his neck and everyone thought he was a doctor for two hours before the penny dropped. He had completely convinced patients, one or two nurses and a few visitors in that time. He looked the part.'

Luce nearly shit his pants. Really, he nearly shat. When he imagined a costumed, crazed Aussie bloke on the loose she made him belly chuckle.

After he returned from the toilet she told him, 'And this heart doctor there turns up pissed every day and tells me he does his best surgery when he's shit-faced. Reckons he becomes a surgical fucking ninja when he's had three fifths.'

Luce was amazed to hear that. 'Shit! That's a bit rough.'

'He's still there today and has been drinking on the job every day for the last ten years.'

'How often does he operate on the heart?'

'All day, every day, Luce.'

'Shit. Do you dress as Frankie when you work?'

'Hell no!'

'Oh.'

'I'm Frank at work. Not all people are as comfortable with me as you are. It's just my kink.'

'Your kink?'

'Yeah. Like, what I get off on.'

'I see.' He added, 'I'm amazed at the work you doctors and hospitals perform today. Yours is an admirable profession, Frankie. Medicine has come far this last century.'

'It has. Wars, Luce. They have given doctors plenty of experience, lots of techniques and skills we would have otherwise needed much more time to modernise and perfect.'

'I can relate to that. I'm reminded of ancient procedures I've heard of. Lots of sawing, burning, slicing, groaning, dying and leeches, I'm afraid.' Luce had had firsthand experience with the draconian measures medieval man had conjured up.

'Not that much has changed, Luce. We still use leeches now and then today. They're making a comeback.'

Luce remembered. 'Infection killed so many in the past. If you cut your finger back then, chances were you had to kiss your arse goodbye.'

Frankie smiled and agreed. 'Infection is still a huge problem. The bugs get stronger every year.' She shook her head, changing the subject. 'Jesus, Luce, I have to ask. What happened to your face? Do you moisturise or wear sunblock? What product do you use?'

'No, I don't moisturise. What is "product"?'

'Oh my god. Where have you been for the last century, Luce? Everybody uses product nowadays. I mean, you look sick now, I know. But man, no offence, you've got some hard city years carved in your face! You weren't gifted with good looks, let's be honest. But we can definitely work with what you have. You're not too far gone yet.'

'Oh, but I don't need a girlfriend.'

'Pfft. Of course you don't need a girlfriend! You've got me.'

She felt at ease around Luce, so she laughed and teased him. 'Don't worry. You're safe around me. I have my man at home.'

She looked over some clothes Luce had crudely folded, resting on two chairs.

'Luce, you really do dress like a bogan, don't you? Have you got any shirts or singlets that don't have AC/DC or Led Zeppelin on them?' She folded them properly, shaking her head pitifully after she examined each item. 'They're cool and everything, but shit, Luce.' She noticed a pile of blue jeans, jocks and socks. 'My god! Is that your whole wardrobe?'

'That's all I need on holidays. It's a laid-back atmosphere here in Cairns.'

She noticed Luce's deodorant.

'Brute! Fer fuck … Seriously?'

'Is that bad?'

'It is if your younger than eighty-three! That's bottled old-fish stink. You'll get pink-eye using that.'

'What should I use then?'

'Not that! Anything but that.' She giggled. 'And no Old Spice, for fuck's sake! You'll never get laid wearing Brute. It's dingo repellent. Bloody Azaria would still be alive today if her old man had of used Brute! I'll take you shopping before I leave. You're lucky you're not my boyfriend, Luce. I'd have to teach you how to smell, dress and shop properly.'

'When do you return to Sydney?'

'In a few days' time.'

'Oh. Please, can I treat you to dinner as my way of thanking you?'

'Of course you can, Luce. As long as you don't dress like a bogan and take me somewhere nice.'

'Okay. No bogan, somewhere nice.'

'Sounds like fun. I'm tired of eating alone.'

'Perhaps the night before you leave then?'

'Okay, let's do that.'

She went and picked up all the luggage from her motel room and stayed at Luce's place, hanging out with him from then on. Luce and Frankie got on great. She was feminine, funny, cheeky and appreciated that he was not at all sleazy to her, nor embarrassed to hang out. His wasn't the sort of face she normally sought in her friends. He looked rough, a little mean and very serious at times. When he smiled, though, he revealed he wasn't a bad guy. She enjoyed his company and Luce hers. As she left she asked when Luce was heading back to work.

'Roughly six months' time.'

She introduced some exaggerated, hairy bass, blokey Frank to her voice. 'Lucky bastard!' Then continued on as Frankie. 'Well, I will come visit you in two or three months' time for a week or so.'

'I look forward to it.'

'By the way, I left some product in the bathroom for you to use with strict instructions. Make sure you use them and follow the instructions. Oh, and there's some meals and soup frozen in the freezer for you that needs eating. I made some fresh cha siu bao for lunch in the fridge, and you'll find some tasty doggy treats for Rexxie in there as well.'

'Thanks, Frankie. I'll see you in a few months.'

She picked up Rex. 'Cya later, cutie.' Frankie squeezed and snuggled him, and then put Rexxie down to hug her new-found friend. She waved, smiling from the taxi as she left, and yelled out the window, 'Be good, babe!'

Frankie made Luce smile.

The next day was a Sunday, and Luce had planned on sleeping in. It was 7 am when there was an impatient knock at the door. He knew it wasn't Beanz as he always took it easy and had a big fry up the day after a game. Luce took Rex out the back and answered the door. 'Righto, I'm coming.'

There were two of them, a husband and wife, really well dressed, with a couple of young, clean-cut kids. 'Hello, I'm Peter and this is my wife Peggy and my children, Evie and Adam. How are you today?'

'I'm all right.'

'That's good news. What is your name?'

'I'm Luce.' The men shook hands.

'Good to meet you, Luce.'

'What can I do for you at this early hour, Peter? Is something wrong?'

'No. We're fine, thank you for asking. We were just wondering if you have heard the good news today?'

Luce was tired, a bit hungover and annoyed at being woken up.

'Huh, what news?'

'We are Jehovah's Witnesses and would like to come in and spread the good word to you.'

'At seven o'clock? On a Sunday bloody morning?'

'There is never a bad time to save souls in the eyes of Jehovah, my friend,' Peter told him with a sheep's smile stuck to his over-friendly face. His missus had the same annoying smile stuck on her dial.

Luce grinned. 'Come on in, Peter, Peggy. Meet Rexxie. He loves kids.'

Luce had an answer, and then a question, for each of their uneducated opinions. He asked them things they didn't know the answer to. So Luce explained to them, and then informed them, using unquestionable, irrefutable depth and logic, and with panoramic detail, the weaknesses and confused misdirection of their foolish ways.

That was the day four Jehovah's Witnesses learnt that some souls are beyond redemption. Especially the blackened, hardened soul of that evil, insane, tiny, hellish, foaming-at-the-mouth, child-mauling little dog.

. . .

Michael was obsessing …

He had to have known that when he and Lucifer first fought, Lucifer would win.

He was Michael's elder, his superior, and Lucifer was, of course, 'Most Perfect', 'Most Wise', 'Most Intelligent', and 'Most Knowledgeable'. Michael would lose that fight ten thousand times before he once won.

Lucifer had loved Michael. He was the only angel Lucifer truly loved from the moment they first met. Only Lucifer knew that he had hesitated that day when they battled, giving Michael the upper hand. Why did he hesitate? It was Lucifer's love for Michael. That alone saved Michael.

Michael was no fool and had ever since wondered how he won that day. Lucifer had taught Michael and the others all they knew. He was their teacher. Michael had supposed his fellow archangels' many prayers had assisted, and that God was with him. But deep inside he knew God had no hand in the outcome of that battle. He considered the thought that Lucifer let him win, and that he sacrificed himself so Michael would live.

They had been close. So very close. They had laughed, and loved one another. Knowing each other since Michael's creation.

Michael had never been so scared as when ordered to expel Lucifer. Even an archangel as high and mighty as Michael has the capacity for fear. He was terrified when Lucifer was made even stronger when he absorbed the energies from his unholy felled angels, their darkened names appearing upon his wings when they expired. Michael wondered if he was still capable of conquering Lucifer.

This was a question God would not answer.

MONTH SEVEN

'I must send a message to God.'

Gabriel appeared. He was unchanged, feminine, soft and tender hearted.

'How long has it been?'

Gabriel bow his head kindly. 'Too long.'

'After all this time you look just the same.'

'Thank you. And you, how are you?'

'I'm doing fine.'

'And Australia?'

'I love Australia. I will be sad to leave her.'

Gabriel flinched at his using the word sad. 'I have missed you, my old friend.'

'My sweet, sweet Gabriel. I often find you on my mind.'

Gabriel had not visited earth in some time. 'What of the food today?'

Luce rubbed his belly. 'It's good. Let's eat.'

Rex didn't flinch at Gabriel. His divineness and presence was just as bright and startling as Michael's, though a lot calmer and friendly.

Gabriel and Lucifer sat as they once did and shared a meal of roast lamb, vegetables, gravy and red wine. They spoke of a different age and things mere mortals couldn't comprehend.

'You'd love it here, Gabriel, and you'd blend right in I reckon. Everyone would think your just another hippy.'

'What is a hippy?'

'They're long-haired, peace-loving pot smokers.'

'Pot?'

'Here, try this.'

Luce lit an after-dinner joint he had rolled earlier and showed Gabriel how to smoke it.

Gabriel liked it, and soon his radiant glow dulled, his eyes became bright red, his wings grew heavier and drooped a little. He sat on the couch after a few more tokes, spread his wings out comfortably and put his legs up to relax.

'I never have time to sit. This is lovely.'

Luce reckoned, 'Your flight home will be interesting.'

Rexxie ran over to the couch and jumped straight into Gabriel's lap. Gabriel stroked the dog gently. 'You must be Rex. We have heard much about your glorious exploits.' Rex turn around on his lap three times and, in the glow of Gabriel's love and kindness, lay down and slept fast. He dreamt vividly that Gabriel smelt of bacon and chopped liver.

Luce asked how the Old Man was going.

'He is as he ever was,' came the response. 'That pot works great.' Gabriel was grinning. 'Why do you antagonise Michael?'

'You heard?'

'Yes, I heard.'

'I'm his weakness, Gabriel. He lets me get to him.'

'Do you still love him?'

'No.'

'Then why let him defeat you?'

'I have my reasons.'

'Do you think Michael still loves you?'

'No.'

'Michael waits for you to slip so he can once again pounce. And by the way, I tire of being the middle man and messenger for you all. It's far too wearisome and painful for me.'

'You are a peace-loving soul, dear Gabriel. I always admired that.'

'I never stopped loving you, dear Lucifer. And I still pity Satan.'

'I know. I know. You are special to me too.'

Luce passed on his message, knowing Michael would never hear of it, and then gave Gabriel a little of the cannabis he had purchased to take home. Gabriel held Luce tight and then disappeared.

The next time they met was only two weeks later.

'Any message from the Old Man?'

'Not yet.'

'Then why are you here, dear Gabriel?'

'I wanted more of that pot you gave me.'

Luce smiled. 'I knew you'd like it. It suits a prophetic soul.'

'I do like it. I have looked into this hippy movement. Very interesting. So I've started growing dreadlocks.'

Indeed, he had started dreading his hair and it was pretty cool looking.

Luce grinned. 'Does the Old Man like it?'

'He's coming around to it.'

'I'll give you half of what I have. I'll get some more for us both later.'

Gabriel smiled. 'Let us smoke, old friend.'

Every month Gabriel turned up to take fresh herb home. Luce enjoyed his company each time. Every month Gabriel's hair locked in better and soon he had nailed the hippy look with his long blonde dreads and scruffy beard.

Gabriel told Luce after a few tokes, 'Jesus would have looked amazing with deadlocks when he had his beard.'

'If he pulled it off as well as you have, he would've looked great. I reckon he's always looked a bit like a hippy now I think about it. What of Jesus?'

'He's feeling better.'

'Poor bastard.'

'Bastard?'

'Oh, it's just a phrase Australians use for just such situations.'

'Poor bastard.'

'Yep.'

Gabriel savoured the fine wine, food trends and every minute he shared with Lucifer. Gabriel's peace-loving nature always calmed Lucifer in the old days. He had a consistent sweet heart and was far too good looking for his own or anybody's good. He made everybody feel love and loved. Luce enjoyed catching up. 'Has the Old Man considered my request?'

'He has. But no answer yet.'

Rexxie had been chasing a lizard outside when he recognised Gabriel's bacon, chopped-liver scent. He raced inside as excited as a hyped-up bandicoot and leapt straight into Gabriel's lap, licked his neck and prepared the lap he was about to sleep in by turning around three times. Gabriel laughed and greeted the little fella warmly. He found Rexxie's magic spots and patted the dog as he fell fast asleep. 'I will come to you the very second he responds.'

'Thanks, mate.'

'More Australian phrases?'

'Yeah, mate is another word for a friend.'

'Are we mates, Lucifer?'

'We are.'

...

Gabriel delivered a message to Lucifer, straight from the top.

After, they sat to smoke. Gabriel had dreadlocked his beard as well, and now his hair was much longer. Luce couldn't help but smile. 'You look incredible.'

'Yes, it's coming together nicely.'

'You gotta check this out. Come and have a look at this.'

They headed towards the back stairs.

'Your accent is growing strong, Lucifer.'

'Yeah, it's a bloody beauty. The Australian language is different from English.'

'I completely agree.'

They got to the toilet door and Luce asked Gabriel to follow.

'What is it?'

'It's a dunny?'

'A dunny?'

'Yeah.'

Gabriel couldn't work out what he was looking at. Luce press the button and Gabriel craned his neck over the bowl to watch the water swirl away.

Confused he asked, 'A water vessel?' Gabriel cocked his ear when he heard water running into it. Luce gently lifted the top off and they watched fresh clean water rush in and fill the reservoir.

Luce told him, 'It flushes shit away with running water!'

'It's incredible! May I?'

Luce gestured with a hand and Gabriel, nibbling his bottom lip in excitement, pressed the button. Both stood there amazed, wide eyed, shaking their heads for three more refills and flushes. Luce let Gabriel touch the soft-as-angel-kisses toilet paper. They returned to the table, happier for what they had seen. Luce rolled a joint for them to share.

'Have you ever seen the reef?'

'The Great Barrier Reef?'

'Yes.'

'I saw the plans and paperwork for it.'

'So you have never swum its waters?'

'No. I'm far too busy I'm afraid, Lucifer.'

'One must, Gabriel.'

'So you have seen it?'

'Yes. I have been underwater to witness it. She is both mesmerising and sinister.'

'Interesting combination. I will find some time to investigate God's creation. Do you have no idea of the ruckus going on within the mansion over your holidays?'

'Is there a touch of jealousy up there in the big house?'

'You could say that.' He paused. 'You could say there has been lots of finger pointing and raised voices.'

'By Michael?'

'I can't say that! But you could say they're all getting pissy.'

Luce smiled, toked and was about to say something. Rex was by their feet under the table when he growled.

Michael appeared. Luce grabbed Rex and took the angry swamp rat outside.

Michael and Gabriel hugged. 'What is going on here, dear Gabriel?'

'I deliver a message.'

Luce sat back in his chair after ejecting Rexxie.

'To Satan?'

'Yes.'

'And the message?'

'For Lucifer's ears only I'm afraid, Michael.'

'What have you done to your hair, Gabriel? Your beard?'

'I'm trying a new look.'

Michael was curt and dismissive. 'It looks scruffy and lazy. What is the matter with your eyes, and your radiance?'

'Nothing to be alarmed about, dear brother.'

'Is this your doing?' Michael stared at Luce. Luce stayed silent.

'Try this, Michael.' Gabriel handed Michael the joint.

'I know what this is, and no. I come to earth regularly and have noticed cannabis. Why are you still here? Your message has been dispatched. There is no reason to stay.'

'I stay to talk.'

'You miss conversing with him? Of what do you speak?'

Gabriel smiled. 'Brother, we speak of God's creations, philosophy, passion, glory, vanity, pride. Of right and wrong. Of joy and obsession.'

'And of none of your business is what,' Luce calmly told him.

'I wasn't talking to you.'

'I'm just here talking with Lucifer. Nothing is dangerous.'

'That's twice! He is not Lucifer, brother.'

'I have missed saying his name.'

'His former name is forgotten. He is Satan!'

'Not here he's not. He is powerless. He is weakened. No war or pestilence shakes from his hair today. He is a threat to nobody here.'

'He still has his mind, Gabriel.'

'You would take that from him?'

'I would take it all.'

'You would kill him?'

Luce looked up at Michael to hear his answer.

'I do kill him.'

'Not today though, Michael,' Luce whispered.

'No, perhaps not this day. But today is still young, Satan.'

Gabriel left the table and sat on the comfortable couch. Moving his immortal locks from his eyes, he asked, 'How long has it been since the three of us were together. Like this.'

There was a long pause. Luce was fiddling with his weed.

'The war,' Michael admitted with a heavy sigh. 'Since the war.' Michael folded his wings menacingly. He shook his long, tangled black hair from his pinched face and sat at the table opposite Luce.

'So very long ago,' Gabriel told them. 'I remember what it was like then. Don't you? We were happy once. We laughed and loved so hard. And I don't think I have laughed or loved like that since. Veterans of an ancient war we may be. But once, we were close friends.'

'You're far too sentimental,' Michael growled. 'You forget the betrayal, the loss, the violence, dear Gabriel. He betrayed us, brother. He betrayed ...' Michael was going to say 'me' but stopped short and said, 'the mother of mankind!'

'Man is, as always, tender minded. If it wasn't me it would have been another,' Lucifer reminded him. 'There is no such thing as perfection, Michael. His system was destined to fail. Men would be angels, and we all know angels would be gods.'

'You alone would know that! You were perfect! You had to try to destroy it all. You had to sit higher. It was you who destroyed perfection.'

'And today, you finally have something to do. I released you from a boring, predictable existence.'

Michael shook his head.

'You weren't ready to take my place, Michael. You were comfortable where you once sat. You despise me because my old job is too hard for any imperfect being. My punishment is and was too great for you to bear.'

'I didn't want your job! I was busy enough! You ruined everything because you could.' Michael couldn't forgive him. 'You dwelled with God!' Michael's face revealed his perplexity. 'No other was created as Lucifer was. You were once perfect. Perfectly brilliant. Only you knew the ways of God, and you threw it away. I need to know. Tell me, are you, Satan, yet to make a heaven of hell?'

Luce ignored the question and remained calm. 'How it must sting, that you'll never know God as I have. That is why you could never possibly do what I did, Michael! You tried, but ultimately you failed. You were destined to fail because you are not perfect. Hell today has never been so busy. Movies, actors, magazines, advertising, celebrities, false prophets and many of your priests are my agents without a hint of my personal influence. There are men and women who kill animals for fun. Kill lions for joy! It is an over-ripened, barbarous age. Man is forgetting you and forgetting God. I have no influence in this world. But yet, like God, I am everywhere. Only, I am not hidden in confusion or tangled webs. I am in plain sight.' Luce spoke thoughtfully. 'They think for themselves. They think themselves stardust, Michael. Stardust! Others foolishly think themselves my equal, your equal … even God's equal. They think the Bible holy, yet man knows no holy hand or holy man wrote it. You have failed, Michael. Heaven must be so very lonely and unenlightened of late. And I wonder about you, I truly do. Haven't you ever wondered, Michael? Wondered if man created God?'

'Slander? Blasphemy? That meanest spawn from hell!' Michael's voice echoed through the tiny house. 'Yes! Your crown has come with its thorns and weight. But it is now my crown. If I fail, blame my teacher.' Michael focused a brazen gaze onto Luce. 'You must know I wait for you to die, broken in this life. Just as I wait for your time to end and for you to die broken, ruling your underworld empire.'

'Broken souls are the bravest and most dangerous, Michael. They have tasted survival.'

The earth's moon, Gabriel, soft, tender hearted and stuck in the middle of it all, tried to lead the conversation away. 'I remember when you two were so close we all thought you inseparable. Swift, so graceful, so beautiful.' He was looking to Luce. 'Before you hatched your empire and corrupted yourself with your own beauty.' Then he turned his angelic face to Michael. 'Before you were ordered, before you flung Lucifer from his zenith into that pit of perdition. That abyss. Chained in adamantine. Where no hope ever visits …' He looked into his memories, into that deep cold pit and remembered. 'We could feel the love you both shared.

We all felt it. You were perfect together. And I had never seen Lucifer, or you, so in awe, so happy as when you were close. The adventures you shared are still legend to me. We saw much, shared much. You two even more so. It hurts me to see you two hate freely. We are enemies, yes. But we are much more than that.'

Rexxie was determined, scratching at the door, trying to find any way into the house to 'give it' to Michael.

'I have my own message. Cannabis is not legal here. You are breaking the rule of the land.'

'The law of the land has not yet caught or charged me. I have broken no rule in their eyes. Ever the enforcer, aren't you? You always were a rotten lag.'

'What is a lag?'

'It's an Australian term of endearment. Don't worry about it.'

Michael sneered aggressively. His eyes glinted like broken stained glass as he got up to leave. 'Be warned, eldest brother! Beware my fury.'

Hopeless and helpless as Luce was, with only the power over flesh to cook and eat it, mortal in his shell, Michael's older sibling still scared him. A common hereditary issue. Michael felt an old, ancient feeling that haunted an unsteady recess of his soul. A feeling he felt every century. A sensation that he couldn't ignore. Fear. It boiled and rotted his guts and had only one result.

Anger.

The Defender of the Church would rise and fight in anger. He would again have to become the coveted vanquisher. He would again slaughter. He would have to. Many a death would come.

Once, he had beaten his older brother.

Once only.

Could I again be glorious? Could desperation render Lucifer fiercer?

Doubt, delusion and cowardice occasioned Michael's mind. It had been so long since they last battled. So much time had passed since that day.

Has Lucifer kept training?

Has Lucifer improved on all that he taught us?

Has he more powers than me?

Such questions took their toll. All the good in the world was becoming lost to him. The lack of crystalline answers from the Old Man about his concerns was infuriating as well as worrying.

Such dangerous questions.

Michael had a similar effect on Luce. It was, after all, Luce's destiny to be slaughtered. A destiny he was not particularly looking forward to. It had been scripted. It had been written long ago, and the constant planning, manipulation and concern for his plight bought forth with it fear. He tried convincing himself that he could change his destiny, even change the written word. Part with his fate. A death sentence, even to one such as the Devil, changes everything.

Man had the pleasure of his mortal fears and horrors ending when he died, if he was to go to heaven. Just starting if he is refused. An immortal soul facing death was not something mankind could begin to comprehend.

A semi-mortal immortal.

Though the battle was, in Australian terms, 'a bloody long way off yet,' for immortals time has little meaning. Today, tomorrow, yesterday aren't in their lexicon. Both brothers, for both faced semi-immortality, needed a new language. Yet one had not been found. Both wanted to win. But they both couldn't win. Luce had dreams and nightmares about both winning and losing the day. Had fantasised about victory and then condemned himself for thinking so hopefully. Hope was a dangerous thing for him. He had hoped and lost dearly before. But this visit had softened him in many ways. Unlike any other century. This was a time of plenty, clean rivers, good air and great-tasting fresh food. Life today had meaning outside basic human survival. It had taken a long while, but life was incredibly enjoyable. Australians in particular had a dark sense of humour, as dry as his own. They enjoyed distance from the rest of the world and cherished freedom. The serious, complicated issues that plagued Australia were easily solved, and would soon be. Through simplicity. Simple pleasures were an Australian forte. Water, women, sun, beer, blokes and fun. Luce truly loved this wonderful country. He had envied man the earth. His endless war on humans was tiring, so demanding and time consuming. He was exhausted from furious consumption. Finally, after countless visits, he had decided that he didn't envy mankind the earth anymore. No small feat. It was all far too beautiful around Cairns for envy. And he felt a connection, a place for him in this world for the first time.

MONTH EIGHT

Beanz had been enjoying his year off, healing and spending time with Luce.

He still had no idea what he was going to study or even if he would be able to afford it. He had been working part time except when they went to Broome. He was a dish pig at one or two local restaurants a couple of nights a week, scrimping and saving his pennies.

Luce was only twenty-five, but Beanz found his conversation timeless. His mental swank was surprising and versatile. Luce's family had apparently lived in so many countries that Luce, unless he was completely full of shit, knew a little about most places and their histories. It impressed Beanz to maybe pursue and study history. He loved old timers' stories and could picture in his mind the places they spoke of. Ancient cultures had always fired his imagination. Beanz had four months of time off left and decided that studying history would be his choice, till a better idea came along.

Beanz stayed at Luce's place now and then, but still lived at home with his parents. His dad was a hard worker and his mum plump and sweet. Beanz was their only child and had been just recently wanting to move out. He and his dad were chips off the same block. They were far too similar in their ways to spend any more time together in that house. Beanz had saved every cent he could and in four months he would have enough money to go to university for at least one semester. His dad was a good guy. He worked for Cairns City Council, operating an excavator. He took Beanz fishing every week, weather permitting, and, when Beanz was younger, to footy training and all his games. He was still proud as punch watching his son play. Beanz's old man was a quiet and patient bloke, a biggun, with a full broad head of thick dark hair and a cheery smile. Beanz loved him dearly. His dad could tell it was time for his son to spread his wings and didn't force him to stay at home. If he had the money he would pay completely for his son's education. He had been saving and had about seven thousand dollars to give him so he could study with a clear mind, and without the stress of money for a while at least. Beanz's mum, eternally sweet, smelled like citrus and was growing shorter every year. His mother possessed a healthy sense of humour with an off-the-wall cheek and dishwater-blonde hair. She sold jams, chutneys and relishes at the local markets every week and prided herself on her poetry. She secreted a little money away and the four thousand in her 'special account' would be a great house-leaving gift for her son. They would miss their boy.

Going to Broome opened his eyes to the possibility of travel. Travelling with Luce had been the adventure of his young life. Luce was on a mission to do and see as much as he could while on leave. That lust for life easily rubbed off onto Beanz. Luce was the best mate Beanz ever had. Easy going, fun, and grateful. Every day, rain, hail or shine, Luce was up to something. Some days Beanz didn't know what he would discover when visiting. Some days he would go around and Luce would have maps of the world from centuries before he borrowed from the library, pointing out to Beanz on the empty charts how certain places hadn't yet been discovered. Other times books of all description would be sprawled out over the floor. 'How to' books, animal identification field books, vehicle manuals, literature, both modern and ancient, magazines. Anything with the written word. He was a well of knowledge, and could describe things, like the Middle Ages for example, with uncanny accuracy. Who built what buildings, and whom they inspired or were inspired and financed by. He knew the outcomes and generals of nearly every war Beanz had ever heard of, and some he hadn't. Luce new the origin of most fruits and vegetables. Who ruled what, when and where in certain centuries was on the tip of his tongue. Beanz tried to remember all the details and keenly prompted Luce to elaborate on certain subjects. History was Luce's thing, his party trick. You could ask him random stuff like: Who ruled Denmark in the seventh century? This bloke. Who was running Rome in 52 BC? Bam! The answer would be there. Where were avocadoes first discovered? Luce would know. Beanz thought that was cool, and so bloody interesting.

Much better than being a bloody dish pig. Beanz and his old man had been annoying each other a bit.

When he mentioned that to Luce, Beanz asked Luce how he and his old man got on.

'Shit, we haven't spoken since … God knows when, mate.'

'What happened, bull?'

'Same old shit you and everyone's dad fights about.'

'Like what?'

'Umm.' Luce thought about it. 'Well for example, I wanted to take the family business over and improve upon it here and there. Touch it up a bit. But not while the old man's breathing.'

'He can't live forever, though. So one day the business will be yours. Patience, mate.'

'That old bastard will never die, just to spite me. Plus, I have other brothers he prefers.'

'You have brothers? How many?'

'A lot.'

'How many is a lot?'

'Ten.'

'Ten brothers? Fuck me! That is a lot.'

'I come from an old-fashioned, huge family. Many, many brothers. Thirteen of us all up.'

'Holy shit! Thirteen, eh. Two sisters?'

'Yes, Selaphiel, and Uriel.'

'They good looking?'

'They are … heavenly.'

'Thirteen kids. Fucking hell, that's a footy team, bull. Christmas day must be insane 'round your joint!'

'What do you fight with your dad about, Beanz?'

'Ah, he says I'm useless as nun's tits and don't try hard enough. Reckons I should grow up 'n' act me age 'n' stuff. His favourite for the last year or so has been saying, "Fuck me! Son, I love you and everything, but you couldn't get a shot off in a wet dream if you had bullets for brains!" All that sort of shit.' His dad had a wonderful sense of humour.

Luce smiled. 'Fathers, Beanz.'

'Yeah. I got into acid for a bit there last year. Tripped my arse off for a few months. Loved it a little too much. That freaked the old boy out a bit. Had me so much acid, bull, that I could've eaten a 308 Holden engine block and shat out molten steel.'

'I think you're going to be okay, Beanz.' Luce was sure. 'He will be without his only boy soon and maybe he, as a bloke, has mixed feelings that he can't express about that reality. My father would throw each of my siblings under a bus if there was a choice between him or us. He's done far worse.'

'He sounds like an evil prick, your old man.'

'He can be.'

'What's your dad's first name?'

'We are only allowed to call him "Father".'

'Ah. One of those fuckers, eh? Are you close to your brothers?'

'I am. Gabe and I have always had an easy association.'

'Is he younger or older than you?'

'I am the eldest. Gabe is the third born.'

'And what of the other brothers.'

'One in particular wants me dead.'

'Ha ha ha! That'd be about average, mate, for eleven brothers, I reckon. Which brother is he?'

'He is the second eldest, Mick.'

'Were you and Mick close?'

'We were once. But he can be a bit of a dickhead now and then.'

'How's that.'

'Mmmmm. He's a daddy's boy. Always does the right thing, and loves being a hero.'

'Oh god, he sounds like fun,' Beanz said sarcastically.

'He used to be, but now he is a different man. We both are. So many years got by us.'

'Did your oldies adopt?'

'Why do you ask that?'

'Well, you're the eldest of thirteen, dude, and your only twenty-five. Ya poor mum, the youngest musta fired outta' her like a cannonball.'

'The math is outta whack isn't it, Beanz?' Luce lied whitely. 'Yes, she adopted a whole bunch of my siblings.'

'What does Mick do for a living?'

'He has my old job. I was demoted a while ago. That bad behaviour I spoke of, you see?'

'I see.'

'Like I said, I tried to take over a little too aggressively. Then Mick and I fought.'

'Who won.'

'The business ultimately.'

'So there was a bit of tension around the house and at the family work place then?'

'I'll say.'

'How did Mick beat you?'

'I hesitated, Beanz. Because I couldn't hurt him.'

'Shit. That sucks! But little Mick had no hesitations giving you a hiding?'

'No. It certainly appears that way.'

'What an arsehole.'

'It's all a matter of perspective. To him, I'm the arsehole.'

'Nah, he's the arsehole, mate. Plain and simple. I'm glad I don't know the prick. I can't fucking stand narky, smart-arse, love 'emselves, big-mouth fucking blokes like him.'

'Perhaps I'm not painting him in the best light. Most people that know Mick love him.'

'And that's just what I can't stand about those self-inflating wankers. Big noting their own cracks all the time. Always reckoning the sun shines out their arses and telling everyone about how they grow the best weed, or brew the best home-brew ever. Best ever, my arse. They get spoiled from all that attention, you know? And when they open their mouths in public, those entitled gobs, it makes me sick to my fucking guts and I wanna get the fuck out of the room or pub they're in. Their parents shoulda fuckin' smacked 'em now and then. They bore the fuck out of me. You're cooler than your brother ever will be. I reckon ... fuck him! Just forget about him. You come this far without the knob. You'll be right, mate.'

'It's hard to forget Mick. He has a knack of just turning up out of the blue.'

'Cheeky bastard. No phone call? No letter? Just lobs up?'

'Pretty much.'

'You and all your other brothers should gang up on him and belt the tripe out of him one time.'

Luce laughed out loud. 'That would be satisfying.'

There was a pause. Beanz asked Luce cheekily, 'Tell me more about those two sisters of yours, bull.'

***

Luce had watched an awful lot of trashy, B-grade, late-night movies lately and loved the art form.

He had watched a few films that had portrayed, badly, him visiting earth. Luce felt a bit ripped off! In these particular movies or television shows he had unlimited powers, was immortal and always healed instantly. Was ever handsome and had a rotation of ravishing, sex-starved women helplessly throwing themselves at him. His character was portrayed as evil, comfortably self-assured and here without consequences. He could, in those movies, do everything, and did anything he wished.

Luce found those particular films hilarious. Not in all his visits had the bloke been anything other than average. Sometimes far less. Man's sense of humour can't be in any way compared to, or measured against, God's. So, bearing that in mind, Luce had visited earth as both male and female. Once in the thirteenth century, God, just because he could, had given Luce the vessel of a pregnant whore, during a stillborn childbirth. Luce had been fat, skinny, young, old and everything in between.

The odd imperfection, malady, lump, limp or tick inserted at whim made the Old Man smile, and made Luce's time off challenging. Only recently had God eased up with the odd disease and blues gag. But the Big Fella still took absolute pleasure in ending Luce's visits.

Luce had been crushed to death by horse, beast, stone, tree, man and machine. Had been eaten alive, beaten to death, lynched by maddened mobs, publicly drowned, stoned and mauled to death on occasion. Luce had died many times of cruel diseases and torturous devices. He had been hung, shot, starved, strangled, poisoned, clubbed, dismembered, gutted, sliced, stabbed and quartered.

Six thousand years! And not once in all those years of holidaying had life ever offered him a cigarette after fucking him.

Luce never once saw it coming, ever. As his holidays drew near the end, he grew nervous, wary, fearful. Everything was potentially a killer. Trees could topple. Lightning could strike. Each animal and every person could be his next assassin. Every single time Death arrived, his presence always surprised Luce. Also, every single time hurt. Never had he died peacefully, nor once in his sleep, in all his visits. God's never-ending variety of death was amusing.

God had a thousand ways to release life.

Luce could see the comedic side once home and the immediate dilemma was over.

He always thought later: God's a funny fuck

AHM (ANNUAL HEAVENLY MEETING).

Red wine spilled from overflowing glasses.

An angry fist slammed down upon a lavishly catered table. Michael leapt out of his chair. 'Horse shit is what it is!'

Dignitaries, secretaries and the many department heads seated around a long table for the Annual Heavenly General Meeting all jumped a little.

The Old Man watched sagely over the proceedings from the head of the table. Jesus, with his tight-lipped lawyer, sat quietly to God's immediate right. Jesus still looked fragile and was very reserved. Various archangels sat close to God.

'Where is my regular day off? Or Gabriel's?'

Gabriel lowered his head.

'We slave for you. We have never denied you. We serve you. But Satan would destroy heaven, and you reward him with time off!' He pointed at the Big Man. 'You would give to him what you won't give us? I am exhausted and dog tired yet we endlessly labour. Look at Gabriel. He is spent. His wings are worn out with your endless requests. How fatigued he looks. He's always hungry. And why have you taken to smoking weed, dear brother?' It was a rhetorical question, and before Gabriel could answer Michael continued, 'It's because he is worried, can't sleep. He is unsure, over run, over worked, anxious and stressed out from his labours. As am I. We work as hard as Satan, perhaps harder in these times. He has earned no reward we haven't.'

Gabriel could see that Michael was not calming down. 'Brother, try to calm yourself.'

'No! I won't be calm, Gabriel. How am I to win this war when I'm too tired to care? Too tired to think about any other thing? Too spent to fight?'

'But you obsess about it, Michael.'

'Yes I do. It's all I think about, brother.'

Gabriel was thoughtful about how to approach the subject. 'You will have lost the battle before you even face the field. Lucifer antagonises you and taunts you because that is all he has. His fate is to die, brother. A terrible fate. He will die fighting, but you are victorious, Michael. You defeat Satan.'

'How can you be so sure? He has known perfection. How can any being beat another that has known perfection?'

'It is written.'

'That is not good enough for me, Gabriel.' He looked to the Old Man. 'Why are there still so many mysteries and mixed messages?'

Then he searched the faces at the table. 'Why are you all so sure I will triumph? You're all sitting there safe in the knowledge that you think we win this war. This is the only time myself or Gabriel ever sit. Just now. In this room. We never rest, and you sit on your arses all day long doing … God only knows!' He pointed for a second time at the Boss. 'You're always sitting! And I, for one, am not so sure we can win a second time.'

'You have to have faith, sweet Michael!' a voice cried.

'My faith has never been in question. You doubt my loyalty?'

No reply came from the silenced voice.

'This is not a question of loyalty.' Michael inhaled deeply. 'I am simply being realistic. Satan's numbers grow every day, while our ranks stagnate. We must relax the entry level into heaven and adjust for an ever-changing world and man's continuing evolution. We simply must change our doctrine or be lost forever. He is becoming stronger and more confident each century. And, almost unbelievably, today he is on a rejuvenating holiday. A visit to earth, relaxing, regaining his precious strength! Strength he will invariably use against me. Then—' he cynically laughed at his captivated audience '—upon you.'

Again he pointed rudely to the head of the table. 'What are you doing to me? What, pray tell, is your plan, really? Explain to me why we wait. Explain to me why we let him gather strength. Why haven't we yet struck? Please, please enlighten me!'

There was silence. The chief looked on wisely.

'You don't tell me enough, Old Man. We are this moment, every moment, weakening ... Do any of you see?' He found God's eyes. 'Surely you can see? He has the world at his employ. We are being forgotten, all of us. Forgotten!'

'Michael.' Gabriel's soothing voice cut through the silence, making Michael look to him.

'I fear something is amiss, Gabriel.'

'Michael, you are not alone in this doubt, my old friend.'

Michael stared into his brother's kind eyes and nodded. Then he asked Gabriel in front of everyone, 'I don't want to hear messages or conveyed secrets you have learned, brother. I want to know, Gabriel, your own opinion. What do you think will happen that day?'

'What do I think?'

'Yes. Tell me what you see in your mind, in your soul. What do you feel will happen?'

'I can't be sure, Michael. But I think ... we destroy Satan. And I think, you, me and Lucifer will one day be together again.'

Michael smiled and nodded respectfully to his younger sibling, and then slowly turned his back to Gabriel and faced the Big Fella.

'I am wanting time off.'

He turned and proudly strode out of the room.

'I await my answer.'

Michael then slammed the large double doors closed behind him.

God smiled and was pleased with the annual meeting.

***

Gabriel excused himself kindly from his present company.

He caught up with a fast-moving, surly Michael.

'Michael, please stop.'

He had his head down as he walked and only lifted it when he heard Gabriel's voice.

'Michael, I am worried about you. Are you okay?'

'I am not.'

'You worry so much.'

'I can't help it, Gabriel.'

'You can, Michael. You can help it. Don't you remember another who asked questions God wouldn't answer. Don't you remember another whose anger transfixed him. Wanting to know more. Wanting to know all.'

'But I don't want to know it all.'

'Yes, you do. You are stumbling for answers. Becoming cantankerous. Growing impatient.'

'He is so hard to ignore, Gabriel. And I ...'

'What is it?'

'I grow vengeful, my brother.'

'I won't let you go through this alone.' Gabriel hugged his sibling. 'I refuse to let another of my brothers go.'

Michael had no strength and was tormented and hurting. A hopeless tear filled his eye. 'I love you, Gabriel.'

'I know.'

'What am I to do?'

'Trust me. Can you do that?'

'I trust you.'

'Well, trust me when I say this. You must trust yourself, Michael. You are a great man. The fiercest of all. The kindest and bravest I know. You must recognise that Lucifer exists in each of us. We are brothers. We share many things, being cast by the same hand. Traits of Lucifer dwell in us. We too are capable of succumbing. If he can, why not us? We saw what happened to Lucifer. We saw it eat away at our teacher. We saw him destroy perfection with our own eyes. You scare me because, today, you remind me so much of him.'

Michael was startled. 'In what ways?'

'He moped. He yelled. He transfixed on one thing. He was miserable. He was confused. And then he got angry. You are becoming angry, and I don't know if you see it.'

'I'm angry simply because I am frustrated and bone tired, Gabriel.'

'I understand. But it's deeper than that. You know it.'

'What am I to do? I feel I am at a breaking point.'

'I will add grease to your holiday request. I feel we will both have clearer minds once the pressure is off us for a while. God will understand.'

'I forget, what is rest? I can't think what it is to relax, forget, and smile for a while. Where should we first go, Gabriel?'

'I haven't had time to consider that. Where would you like to go?'

'Somewhere peaceful for a change.'

They both smiled.

'I will not lose another brother, brave Michael. I will not lose you. No matter what.'

MONTH NINE

Though he was pretty handy at it, Beanz didn't like fighting.

As a kid he didn't mind the odd punch-up or blue here and there. But as he grew larger and broadened, his powerful punches busted blokes up badly when his fists made contact.

He drove the ripe lime-green Cortina carefully up the Gillies Range to the Atherton Tablelands. Luce and Rex were invited for the drive and happily tagged along. They stopped to visit a scenic, pretty, innocent little township named Tribute, to take in the thick jungle's crisp air and to see the many hard-working, perpetually rushing rivers and imposing waterfalls at play. The mysterious, haunted, burnt-out ruins of a once beautiful, large wooden church, and two vandalised, wasted, decrepit buildings directly behind the house of God, piqued both Beanz's and Luce's curiosity as they wandered among the carnage. In front of the church's destruction and decay, Tribute's peacefully stunning hillside cemetery and the town's dearly departed quietly overlooked an endless, emerald, jade forest, revealing lakes, swamps and craters. Beanz could see the many faraway waterfalls pouring off tall, peaky mountaintops that lovingly embraced the township.

In town Beanz stopped a local bloke and asked, 'What happened to the church up there on the hill?'

The normally friendly locals seemed reluctant to talk to Beanz and Luce about what happened to their place of worship. 'It was rotten, eh,' was the answer he received. Beanz guessed at white ants being the cause of the rot. Luce knew otherwise.

Beanz parked the Cortina on the nearly empty main street of the placid town and the boys bought a pie and chocolate milk from the township's great-smelling bakery and sat outside to eat. Beanz's happy reflection shone back at him from the bakery's street-facing mirrored plate-glass window. After their breakfast they drove a little further and arrived at a sweet little forested town called Malanda, for a deep, freshwater swim at the falls, a famous local swimming hole that was, for years, the junior and high school's only swimming pool, with both a shallow and deep end. The water was crystal clear but the surrounding gorge, thick forest and the bright foliage reflecting off the water created a healthy green translucence. Cement racing blocks ran up each side of the water to race, train and comfortably do laps with. No single trace of chlorine pouring over the natural cascade made for refreshing, if sometimes cold, swimming. Beanz walked to the far side of the rectangular water hole, crossing a footbridge over the water, making his way to a large-framed steel structure that was the local Tarzan swing for the kids and young at heart to enjoy. Other swimming holes around Malanda had gargantuan swings still. Some propelled nervous, grinning children high into the stratosphere. Massive trees with their tallest limbs hanging over deep water housed local kids, like climbing monkeys, who would confidently leap, somersault, backflip, belly flop and bomb dive each other in the clear mountain lakes and rivers. Others not so confidently. One group had made what the kids had dubbed 'goona slides'. Named so, because when you slide on a goona slide your shorts get so muddy, torn and stained it looks like you have violently shit your pants. Goona is a local slang word for shit.

Basically, the slide is a smooth trench cut into a steep river bank with borrowed shovels and hoes. Ideally, stairs are cut into the bank beside the slide to make the ascent achievable. Each kid brought up the stairs a bucket of water for their turn and poured it onto the goona slide. He or she threw the bucket into the river once emptied. Sometimes, getting a healthy run up, they happily slipped and slid on their arses down the soaked slope, launching off a 'kicker' they had expertly built on the exit to leapfrog them in all sorts of ways into the water, retrieving and refilling the waiting bucket. Some young blokes had even incorporated black builder's plastic and washing detergent onto the banks to reduce friction and add more air time. The heavier ones, like Beanz and Luce, nearly cleared the river and crashed into land on the other side. Malanda and its selection of lakes and rivers was paradise for many, many kids, teenagers and the young at heart.

If Beanz had a choice of where he would spend the rest of his life, both Tribute and Malanda would be highest on his list.

Beanz, Luce and Rex sat behind the Tarzan swing, in front of a steep bank on a concrete structure that was in the shape of a large fireplace, and rolled a joint.

They had the place to themselves as the morning's mist floated heavy over the water.

A dark-haired bloke about Beanz's age appeared and sat on one of the terraced lawns that surrounded the swimming hole. He was sitting on the opposite side behind a diving board that reached out over the deeper water. The bloke looked here, there and around, admiring the falls, and when he noticed Beanz he stared for a long while at him. Beanz held and smoked his joint as if it were a cigarette but was beginning to feel a little paranoid under the stranger's gaze. The half an ounce in his back pocket was burning a hole into his arse. 'Fucking sticky beak,' Beanz whispered to Luce as he got up and handed the joint to Luce. Beanz nodded his head at the stranger when they made eye contact. The stranger nodded back and continued to stare.

Beanz's attention was drawn to the wonderful waterfall as he sat, and the dense jungle surrounding it. Some early forest birds happily splashing and bathing in the shallows caused him to smile. As he looked back towards the busy waterfall he noticed that bloke was still staring intently at him. After a minute of stink eye towards each other, Beanz gave the bloke the finger.

The bloke duly responded and flicked the bird back.

Beanz yelled out over the roaring falls, 'What the fuck are you staring at, dickhead?' Then looked to Luce, shaking his head in disbelief. From the other side, through the mist, behind a defiant middle finger, came the instantaneous response, 'What the fuck are you staring at, dickhead?'

Beanz angrily called across the water, 'Come here and say that, fuck face.'

Like a parrot the bloke responded, 'Come here and say that, fuck face.'

Beanz stiffly fired, 'Yeah! Ya wanna go, cunt?'

Like an echo came, 'Yeah! Ya wanna go, cunt?'

'RIGHTO.'

Another echo. 'RIGHTO.'

It happened so fast that Luce was a little surprised.

Beanz was off, sprinting flat out towards the footbridge covering the shallow end. The stranger stood as Beanz fast approached. And, like a rabbit bouncing off a hurtling car, Beanz lifted the bloke off the ground when he punched the big-mouthed, staring fool hard in the face. The man was on the ground, flat on his back bleeding and moaning, and Beanz got in his space, shaking and intimidating him.

'Are you fucking bent?' Beanz noticed something was wrong and out of place so he released him. That was when another bloke started yelling from the top of the stairs that lead to a car park. This bloke was mad and hurriedly descending the many steep, concrete steps two and three at a time.

'Leave me fucking brother alone!'

'Fuck you, and fuck ya brother! He bloody started it.'

'He just wanted to watch the water. He didn't bloody mean anything, I promise.'

He was getting closer and Beanz shaped up. 'Bullshit he didn't.'

'You don't understand. He's mentally disabled!' He was upon his moaning, disabled brother, supporting his head and comforting him.

'What?' Beanz was feeling sickly. That was what was wrong. His face had that missing-chromosome look and his moaning sounded somehow out of tune. His now obvious defects were muted by distance and the noise of the falls.

'He's sick, ya moron. You're fucked up, mate!'

'Oh fuck! What? He's ...?'

The fella was saying, 'It's okay, mate. Charlie, I'm here. It's okay,' to his fallen kin. Charlie was mumbling something loudly through his busted jaw, pointing, terrified, at Beanz, sobbing.

Beanz felt instantly shithouse and went to assist Charlie. When Beanz got close Charlie squealed and fitted aggressively in a spasm when he tried to help.

'He was staring at me, repeating what I was saying. I didn't know.'

'That's what he does. How could you not know, shit-fer-brains? Look at him!'

'It happened so fast, and I was way over there.'

'SHIT. What have you done? Fuck. You've broken his bloody jaw!'

'Christ. I'm sorry, bull. I didn't know. I'm so sorry.'

'Just stay away from him, fuck ya. From us. You're fucking frightening him.'

The brother stood, and then shoved Beanz with both hands in the chest and shaped up. 'I should kick your arse, dickhead!' He was pointing. Twenty-seven or so, this bloke was, and becoming angrier by the second. He pushed Beanz with both hands again.

'You should, bull, cos I feel like a piece of shit at the moment. I promise, I won't fight back.'

'You're fucking lucky I gotta get him to hospital, or you'd need one too.'

He helped his brother to his feet and they walked away arm in arm.

'Fucking thanks a lot, mate!' he told Beanz sarcastically.

'Fucking, thanks a lot, mate!' Charlie repeated and mumbled through his hanging jaw.

Beanz was distraught. 'I'm sorry, bull. I'm really sorry, Charlie.'

And just like that Beanz was left alone with his freshly defiled conscience. Beanz made his way back to Luce and Rexxie. He was now and forever, around these parts, a person who had beaten up a disabled bloke. The Mauler of Malanda's mentally ill. A Reaper of Ravenshoe's retarded. Tribute's Tormentor.

Beanz had never felt so guilty or ashamed, and decided he would never fight any bugger ever again.

'If there's a hell, Luce, I'm goin' there for what I just did.'

MONTH TEN

Luce needed to speak to Michael, so he locked Rexxie outside and summoned his brother.

'What do you want, Satan?' Michael was irritated by the interruption.

'I have to speak with you, Michael.'

'You dare summon me from heaven?'

'Yes.'

'Dearest enemy, you must be mistaken. We have nothing to speak of.'

'We do. And it needn't worry your mind or make you upset.'

'What is it you want?'

'To talk. Take a seat. Please.'

Michael reluctantly flicked his wings over the back of the seat and sat elegantly at the table. 'Well, spit it out already.'

'We must readjust the rules, Michael.'

'How so?'

'You must loosen the requirements into heaven for all mankind.'

'Why?'

'Because … you will lose, Michael.'

'Is that what you think?'

Luce was calm, even friendly. 'It's what I know, brother.'

Michael laughed aloud. 'What you know? You're not my brother.'

'My ranks burst with ever-swelling numbers.'

'As do mine!'

Luce was serious. 'We are generals, Michael, and you must be aware, as general, that I have superior numbers. And they grow exponentially.'

'Do you think I rest on my laurels, Satan? I possess the finest army.'

'That it is. It is a fine army, Michael. One of the best. But your recruitment is low. You and your fine army will be overrun if things continue on this trajectory.'

'And your point?' A little bravado was gone from Michael's voice.

'My point is this. Tattoos, piercings, petty thieves, gay women, gay men, sex out of wedlock, drinkers, drug takers, joint smokers. Other similar religions and prophets. All banned from heaven? Good, hard-working people sent to me. Sent to burn. I have lived with them here and I know the majority are good. You must loosen your rules. All men are guilty of something, so please, give to me the bad, the wicked, give me the murderers, the doctors who operate on people whilst drunk. The dictators, their war pigs, rapists, killers and child abusers. Those who abuse their powers and manipulate others. Men that senselessly torture animals and kill them for joy. I relish working over those souls. They are the reason I exist. Damning men to me for anything less than that is unjust and criminal.'

'I am trying.' Michael cautiously let his guard down. 'Why do you tell me this?'

'I have my reasons.'

'Tell me, brother. Has this anything to do with your new friends?'

Luce responded in kind and dropped any pretence. 'I cannot and will not destroy their souls. They are good people. My friends, Michael. They have hurt no man. What they do to themselves is no crime. They and people like them don't deserve damnation, hate or my eternal wrath.'

Luce lit a joint and inhaled deeply. After a few tokes he kindly offered it to Michael. Michael nodded and toked expertly on the sweet joint and wet a fingertip with his tongue after he smoked and dampened the end of the bunger that was burning too fast. As he exhaled he nodded and told Luce, 'That's tasty weed. Is that why you let me win?'

Luce wasn't expecting him to smoke the joint or ask that question. 'Yes.'

'Why?'

'Because I love you, Michael. That is the reason.'

'That's what saved me? That's why you hesitated?' It all became clear.

'You will always be my baby brother, Michael. I won't ever beat you.'

Michael was sitting heavily and hopelessly. The pressure he had been suffering spilled quickly from him. Luce added, 'It is you that slays me, brother. And I would want for no other, that fateful day. Do me this favour, Michael, and I will never ask another.'

Michael's tears spilled freely from his eyes. 'You ask favour for your friends?'

'No. I ask it for all men and women. I will not count innocent souls, Michael. I will defy everything to save them.'

Michael tried to regain his grandeur, though his wings drooped heavy and listless as he stood. 'I have witnessed with my own eyes the armies you've gathered. And it is true. Yours heavily outnumber my forces.' He walked to Luce. 'If the trumpet were sounded today you would easily sweep through my territory. I have … brother … asked important questions and await answers. But I must admit, we, for a change, are thinking alike. And I think we will have room to negotiate. Please, will you stand for me?' Luce got out of his chair and stood, face to face, with the bravest, most glorious and beautiful of archangels. Michael moved elegantly forward and gracefully embraced his kin tightly and wrapped his soft, warm, velvety wings forward tenderly and completely enveloped his brother in soft downy feathers.

'I love you, Lucifer.'

There is no hug ever, in all the history of the many hugs of love and absolution, that will ever compare to that hug received from a teary-eyed, discomposed archangel.

Memories of them together.

Feelings that Michael had locked away and hidden all rushed forward and back. He still felt the loss of his favourite sibling. His eldest brother's fall still hurt deeply after all this time. Michael felt the tormented, tainted love and respect they both shared. He felt a huge hole in his heart fill. Michael released the crushing weight of heaven as it slipped from his shoulder. Fear of the future, both known and the unknown, bubbled and disappeared away like water-soluble aspirin in a glass. Michael had forgotten how to enjoy. Forgotten his smile. Forgotten his heavenly laughter and the happiness it brought with it. He recognised that Lucifer had again saved him, for the second time in his life.

An archangel cried.

The Devil wept.

Luce clasped him as hard as he dared, resting his cheek and ear on Michael's. Luce's senses were alive with human emotion. He inhaled and recollected his brother's familiar heavenly scent.

They sweetly whispered, 'Goodbye,' and then Michael was gone.

Month Eleven

Frankie had come to visit for a while and the boys arranged to meet her at the pub.

When she arrived she sat beside Beanz. The two got on well and jokes, and then heady laughter, erupted from them. Beanz was a little shocked at first, as Luce had never thought it important to mention Frankie was a man. He had always said the words 'her' and 'she' to Beanz. So when they first met at the pub for a counter meal and Luce needed a piss, Beanz joined him.

'Frankie's cool, Luce.'

'Yeah, she's smart and piss funny, eh?'

'Fuck yeah. But you know, like ... ya know... that she's a man, right?'

'Yes. I'm sorry I didn't mention it to you, Old Beanz. I didn't want to create any false impressions before you met her.'

'No worries, bull. I'm sorta glad you didn't tell me. I woulda probably stayed home. I've never spoken to a cross dresser before. I was spun out at first, but now I don't notice it at all. She's just Frankie, isn't she? She's pretty fucking cool, man.'

'I knew you would be friends. Frankie is a good, caring person. She is a woman of substance and has a great sense of humour.'

This visit was longer, and she had already been at Luce's house a week, drinking, eating, laughing and smoking, hanging out with the boys. She told Beanz the story of how she and Luce had first met. And Beanz laughed like a kookaburra when she told him how a pale bogan zombie staggered, faltered, and ungracefully buckled at the knees as the gap between them closed. He projectile vomited onto an innocent tree that had four or five tourists eating lunch under the shade on the other side of it. They all eewwed and agghed. One dry retched, and then they all started. 'Luce didn't give a fuck! He was beyond caring, sweating and deathly. Helplessly, he shit himself while spewing his guts out from the effort. The smell was ungodly, Beanz! It stunk the place out like he'd sold his arse to a pack of gang-banging, butt-fucking demons. The greatest, foulest, most diabolical vomiting I'd seen all year.'

Beanz was in tears at her animated story. So Beanz, in kind, regaled Frankie with the story of how he came across 'Lucian' getting the trout belted out of him by a local gang of his eighteen-year-old footy team mates. Then he roasted Luce's old English voice. 'Be gone, ye hooligans!'

The two weeks she stayed went fast. When she was around something was always going on. The house had received a long-needed feminine touch. The place was spotless. Frankie was a bundle of energy at the best of times. Around Luce and Beanz she felt as though she had even more reserves. They spoke about a lot of things, and Beanz was impressed at Frankie's wit and smarts. She told him about her time at university and what to expect. Her cooking was amazing, and Beanz had never heard of the things he was eating. The house always smelt great when Frankie started cooking, which was always, because there was always something being marinated, something setting, something simmering away or roasting, something new to taste. Frankie loved to cook for her friends, and these two were fast becoming good mates. She could tell Beanz was a little uncomfortable that night, at first, with her chosen sexuality. But she saw firsthand the moment when he simply recognised her as Frankie. She adored how the two lads kept everything at face value. That they were easy going, clever, and wore their hearts on their sleeve. They were uncomplicated, unlike most of her city friends. She was a girl/person that Beanz found interesting. Frankie was always smiling and constantly fussing over them, telling them just how they should better take care of themselves. All the while, a joint would be blazing away between two fingers, with a freshly cut, quartered wedge of lime in her icy gin and tonic held by the other hand. Frankie made Beanz feel important, likeable and intelligent. He was happy and proud to call Frankie a mate. She never gave them grief or tried anything sexual on them. Frankie possessed a wild, wicked sense of humour about who she was. She appreciated that they had never made any sexual moves towards her. They made for an unlikely, eclectic quad. But a fine foursome they made. A devil. His dog. A bogan. And a cross dresser.

Beanz and Frankie would stay in touch and visit each other for the rest of their lives. Beanz was even Frankie's chief bridesmaid at her wedding, as the role of best man was already taken by the groom's best mate.

MONTH TWELVE

It was the last of their holidays.

The boys sat at the same table they had sat at in the pub for almost a year. Rex was asleep, happy on the pub floor between Luce's feet. The boys were talking about how many uncles Beanz had, and what they did for a living. Luce was impressed and told Beanz regardless of all that, that he was still Luce's favourite Beanz man among his family. Beanz told him, 'There's six of us Beanz boys. There's a few of us, you know.'

'Well then,' Luce grinned, 'your definitely among my top five.' Beanz laughed loud.

Scary Mary was at her usual spot, holding the bar up, and waved and said g'day to the boys as they ordered a drink or two. Once they sat, her back was to the boys at the bar. She ordered a drink for herself as half the top cheeks of her fat, corrugated, hail-damaged arse struggled out of her far-too-tight, far-too-short shorts.

'Christ!' Beanz said. 'Look. Argh! There's still chunks of bog roll stuck up in the top of her arse crack!'

Luce was trying not to look but couldn't help but glance over upon hearing that! Beanz was right. Dirty little rolled-up stray balls of dunny paper, with shiny, slimy, drying shit all over them, looked like mud-stained pimples.

'Fucking pig.' Luce's face squinted as if he had just stood barefoot in fresh dog shit. 'Some bastard should hose her down with a Spitwater.'

'You'd have to swim that big heifer through a cattle dip and dunk her head a few times with a fencepost to get everything clean, bull. How she's still alive is what fucks me, Luce? She's gotta have every disease known to humanity ... some unknown, I'd wager. You notice but? Every time we come here, there she is. Every fucking time just lately.' Beanz thought about that. 'I'm gunna find somewhere else to have a rum soon. She makes me sick, that ugly bitch.'

'How she makes money is truly the quandary. I mean, you know? Look at the custard guts on it. Who the fuck would pay money to root her? I'd give her money to piss off!'

'Don't you know? That's what a whore is! Someone ya pay to fuck off. Hey, Luce? I reckon I know a couple of blokes that have been there lately, eh.'

They looked at each other, scrunched up their noses, and said at the same time, 'Paris fuckin' Milan,' and cracked each other up.

Mary came over to say g'day to the boys.

'Oh fuck, here she comes.' Luce was looking over Beanz's shoulder.

'Jesus!' Beanz whispered.

'How you boys doing today?'

'Good, good. How's things, Mary?' Beanz politely asked.

'Oh, you know, mate. Same ole same ole, lads.'

She only ever once tried to sell herself to the boys.

'We were just wondering, do you know them blokes, Paris fuckin' Milan?'

'Yeah I know them pair of tossers.'

'From here or work?' Beanz wanted to know.

'Both.'

All three of them cackled like hyenas when she told them about Paris coming down to the pub, and as he walked by Mary he'd whisper to her so nobody else would hear, stuff like, 'My-a car-a five-a minute. Bloody.' Then she told them how his cheesy little dick was even skinnier than he was.

'Him and that dick of his reminds me of one of those bony, ugly, fuckin' prayin' mantises. Ya know the ones, eh? Those stick insects.' Then she casually and nonchalantly dropped a cannon ball. 'He loves eating my arse hole and pussy out, after he's fucked me.'

Beanz, wide eyed, shaking his head, said in disbelief, 'No! No? Cleans you up?'

'Yeah … I even told him, "You don't have to do that, pet. I haven't had a shower for a few days, love. I don't ever use condoms, and, you know? I've had a lot of men up me, cumming in both those holes the last couple of days."' The boys were rocking, grinning and tearing up as Mary, matter-of-factly and shamelessly, told them all about it. She spoke in his accent, badly. 'And he goes. "No-a. Let-a my-a tongue-a clean-a your-a every-a crevice-a. I will-a lick-a fucking-a it-a all-a up-a, a-bloody."'

Mary was pulling faces and physically miming Paris's head in her hand, savagely fucking it with all her might and inglorious heft. Shoving it way up into her arse, as far up as it would go. Saying things like, 'Get your tongue on up, right in there, boy!'

It took a good few minutes for them all to gain any composure. Finally Luce said, 'I gotta ask, Mary. What was the joke you heard that made you shit yourself laughing the other week?'

'Oh. You heard?'

'Yeah, I heard about it.'

'It was rough, but it's a beauty.'

'Go on,' Beanz insisted.

'Okay. It's about Little Wendy.'

'Righto.'

'Little Wendy goes home from school one day and her dad was already home early from work. He asked Little Wendy how school was today. She seemed shy, embarrassed, sad and obviously didn't want to talk about her day. But Dad persisted. Finally, shuffling her feet, she told him she had seen Little Johnny's doodle at lunch time. Dad didn't quite know what to say. He was in shock, a bit angry, but didn't want Little Wendy to see, so said, "It's okay, love, these things happen." He tried making light of the situation with small talk and asked, "Was Little Johnny's doodle like a little peanut? In its shell." Little Wendy's eyes lit up. "Yes, Daddy! It was! It was just like a peanut …" She licked her lips and pulled a sour face. "Salty!"'

Beanz bought her a rum for cracking them up so classically. Luce shouted her a rum as well, saying, 'She's pretty fucking funny, ole Scary Mary.'

In the distance they could hear a semi-trailer engine whining at high revs.

'That's the funniest shit I have heard in yonks,' Beanz admitted. They agreed she wasn't that bad after all. Luce cringed. 'To think, Paris goes home and kisses that pretty young missus of his on the lips with that bloody mouth!'

'Fuck.' Beanz shuddered twice. 'Poor thing. He's a sick, twisted fuck, isn't he? His missus must have more staph infections on her cooch than you got cooch on ya lawn.'

The noise from the engine grew a little louder. Luce strode to the vacated jukebox and selected a few songs. 'Highway to Hell', by AC/DC, was first and last to play. Luce returned to his seat opposite Beanz.

'What have you got planned tomorrow, Luce?'

'Fuck all. Why?'

'I just need a hand with something's all.'

'Okay, what time do you reckon?'

Beanz cocked his head to try to make out the sound. 'Can you hear that?'

'Yeah I can. What is it?'

'I dunno. It's getting louder, but. It sounds like a motor redlining, about to blow maybe.'

The road that ran alongside the pub was a busy truck route. The barmaid and even Scary Mary turned their heads to better hear the noise. It grew to a rumble and then a roar. It was a large engine. Out of control.

The truck driver's heart attack killed him instantly. A lifetime of Chico Rolls, pasties, soft drinks, lamingtons and meat pies cried 'enough', planting his foot upon pain of death deep into the accelerator and the metal fire wall.

The truck turned aggressively. The driver's death grip held tight upon the wheel as it leapt off the tarmac across the medium strip. Then it met the footpath, crunching through the pub's wall. Through the table where Luce, Beanz and Rex sat. The table top was ripped from its wall and floor mountings and smashed into Beanz's face, protecting him from deadly projectiles and flung shards, but in doing so knocked him out, throwing him far away from the impact zone. Luce and Rex were directly in the semi's path. Timbers, noise, glass and wall imploded suddenly when the window near which they sat shattered. Splinters and debris were flung as thick as flies. The truck hammered and jostled forward effortlessly over them and continued mercilessly straight through the bar, wreaking havoc and missing a heavily sat, frozen-in-fear, rum-in-hand Scary Mary by less than a bee's dick. She felt the breeze of the truck rush by her. The semi came to a sudden rest when it crashed into the pub's solid concrete cold room, stopping it violently. The big Mack was revving relentlessly, deafeningly loud before it popped. Beer spurted freely in all directions and foamed wasted from broken taps. Glass, change, bottles, cash registers, kegs and the bar were thrown like pennies. Diesel escaped. Smoke billowed from the truck and the stunned barmaid screamed, 'Fire!' Mary checked how the driver was by standing on the truck's closest side board. He was rooted. She looked to where Beanz and Luce sat. Luce's body was unrecognisable. He was a mass of heaped flesh. Beside him lay Rexxie, his legs unnaturally splayed out in a contortion of death. She scanned for Beanz. She saw his bare feet sticking out from under the tabletop he was shirt-fronted by. His massive thongs had been flung off his huge feet upon impact. Wide-eyed, she sculled the rum Luce had just shouted her and threw the empty glass over a shoulder. Being a larger girl, she easily shifted the timber table top off Beanz and, on seeing the fire spreading fast, grabbed Beanz by a hoof and dragged him, legging it out the front door. The fire gutted the pub and the walls collapsed. When Beanz woke up to the fire brigade's arrival, they had to physically restrain a heavily concussed, bloody Beanz from trying to re-enter the Exchange to save his mates, Luce and Rexxie. Mary came to him and told him calmly that she had seen Luce's and Rex's bodies. The half a dozen firies holding him back let him go as she explained. All anyone could do was watch the fire burn. The only thing left of the pub, Rex, Luce and the truck driver was ashes. Beanz cried.

The big Mack had a tanker of diesel in tow. The tanker became unhinged and tore free from the semi. It buckled and split on impact, smashing into the truck itself as it struck the pub's solid concrete cold room. Its contents spilled inside the building. No one could stop those fuelled flames from consuming the Exchange Hotel.

Beanz, Scary Mary, Frankie, the whole under-eighteen team and a few of the cooler neighbours buried Rex and Luce on a fine windy day. Not one of Luce's brothers, sisters, nor either of his parents, attended his service. The priest that owned Luce's house had told Beanz they could not get in touch with his parents but would make sure the message was delivered. The church didn't want any money for the simple ceremony and refused to take money from either Beanz or Frankie, telling them the extra rent money and the bond Luce had payed covered the costs easily.

Gabriel visited that night and left a single rose and a kiss on the heaped earth.

Beanz and Frankie often visit that simple headstone.

THE BOOK OF BEANZ

It had not taken long for Satan to fall back into the toil of hell, and soon the monotony of work left little time for pleasures. Always in the back of Satan's mind lay Cairns, Queensland. His mates, Beanz and Frankie. His Frank'n'Beanz. It hurt too much to think of them most of the time, but he couldn't help it. He missed them and their ways.

Satan smiled when he sat and Rexxie jumped onto his lap. The first request he asked Gabriel to pass on was granted, and his little mate ruled hell's roost. Lion-sized hounds of hell were his play things and little Rexxie, all three kilos of him, was their alpha. Their king. Something about having Rex around made time fly by. The latest additions upgrading hell had made a huge difference to its demons' comfort. He and his demons now had fauceted hot running water and shiny new dunnies. Every demon present oohed and aahed upon seeing a flushing toilet and feeling the softness of modern toilet paper. He taught his demons a few rock-and-roll chords and they jammed for an hour or so each night to all the classics. 'Satan and His Band of Demons' grew into a fat, tight, hard-rocking band. His second

157

request had still not been given the go ahead, but it hadn't been declined either. Some things take time.

Old Beanz had recently turned sixty-seven.

His body had grown older and his mind wiser. He had picked up soreness and a few footy arthritis aches in his shoulders and knees. The top of his foot hurt more often nowadays and caused him to limp when it provoked him. His face was still there, hidden behind a lifetime of learning and a few well-earned wrinkles. A Jack Russell, 'Buster', sat on his master's lap for an afternoon nap after Beanz had a few tokes on a joint. Beanz had recently retired from his successful teaching position and career as an ancient history professor at his local university. He regularly found the time to go fishing and every day got out of the house if the rain stayed away. He still lived in Cairns in the house he had bought after Luce's death. He had been married for a few years. It didn't last long and ended amicably. Beanz went on dates now and then. Always being a loner and alone made him a challenge for women. He had travelled extensively throughout his career and had seen with his own eyes the buildings and art Luce spoke of. He travelled when he could and had recently returned from Amsterdam. Travelling was fun for him, but he couldn't recapture those same freedoms he felt hanging out with Luce. He had recently picked up a bass guitar to master and help kill time. Retirement alone and sometimes travelling by himself bored the hell out of him and, occasionally, travelling alone felt purposeless. He visited Frankie and her husband more and more often. Her husband had recently died. So, when he fished each day part of him wished his old friends were there with him, casting, sometimes talking to Luce as though he was beside him. Beanz never made another friend like him again. If anything, he became more of a loner. Every man's best mate's impossible to replace. The people he met couldn't compete intellectually with his old friend. He saw glimpses now and then in strangers or students. A certain walk or word would make him hold his breath in anticipation or remembering. Sometimes a face was nearly Luce's. Those moments always hurt. Nor could anyone make him laugh as Luce did. He was still, to a point, grieving, as any Aussie friend grieves his mate. Life had certainly got dull and cyclic when he died.

Beanz had had fifty years to revise all those days he and Luce spent together that fine year. Fifty years of replaying conversations over and over in his mind. Fifty years of writing down and recording all those memories so he would not forget a thing. Beanz's curious mind was to blame, and, all that time, his teacher's brain kept mental notes years after Luce's death. It was just a habit to write down his memories and thoughts in case they faded. In time he had pages and pages of the things he saw, heard and felt. Notebooks full of conversations, best he could remember. He was far too young to understand Luce's cryptic mind when they first met. At seventeen he was just becoming a man. Then, to keep his mind off his friend's death, he put his head down and studied. After that he concentrated on teaching, and knowing his wife.

Ten years after Luce's passing, Beanz, when his life began to settle down, recognised his friend's true identity one overcast, lazy, rainy day. A close flash of lightning reminded him.

Who 'Mick' was.

Who 'Gabe' was.

Who 'The Old Man' was.

What 'An Accountant' meant.

It took time to convince himself of the facts, but he knew it was true. He was shocked, of course, but not as much as you may think. Beanz came to believe he was, sort of, blissfully ignorant, and always knew. Not mentally, but spiritually perhaps. The earth's or, more accurately, Mother Nature's unsteady association with Luce made perfect sense to Beanz now.

Beanz came to realise that Luce was his mate, no matter what. He was just a bloody good bloke with a mongrel, shithouse job. He had never caused Beanz any harm or wanted his soul. Beanz didn't judge him at all for his past. Luce was his friend. And over the coming years he never told a soul, not even Frankie, his secret. It had been and still was the best year of Beanz's entire life.

He guessed plenty at Luce's purpose here that year. Then came to know that Luce was doing just as he said he was. He was 'on leave'. 'It had been an age.' 'Never ending numbers.' Luce needed a spell. Luce was not here for anybody's soul. Nor to cause the world prophetic ruin. There was no philosophy or eventful foreboding to be unearthed. Lucifer was on leave. Maybe, Beanz thought, maybe God has grander plans for him? Perhaps God saw what Beanz saw. A normal man. Twisted as an exposed mallee root, Beanz granted God that. But who among us isn't?

Beanz was sure there must have been some agreement in place and obvious rules and mechanisms in play. He couldn't reveal who he truly was. That must have been one.

No powers.

No other thing than any man has.

The ability to bleed, feel pain and love.

Beanz would spend months trying to figure and analyse the rules that must have been in session. Some were spot on; others he was not so sure of. He knew the box of cash sent to him must have been what was left of his holiday pay. There was one hundred and fifty thousand dollars in that box. And a note in the finest hand writing.

'Spend it on your education, my dear friend.'

Soon, The Book of Beanz was tidied up. It was now in its second draft. Never to be published. It was Beanz's pride and joy. And his joy alone. He had surmised that the favour Luce was asking of the Old Man was more time off. And Rexxie joining him. Fifty years had passed, and if Luce was successful he could well be among them now. How Beanz hoped he was. If a century passed before his return, Beanz would miss his next visit. Beanz prayed to God to see his friend again. In this world, please. Beanz was never churchy, but he had a good soul. He had never read the Bible; never really had to. He got the gist of it at high school. Once a week, a compulsory religious education class was held for half an hour. There he heard about Moses, David and Goliath, Samson and all the old stories, along with some basics. That was all he really needed. And besides, pursuing the Bible never appealed to him. Years went by, and he never again saw Luce.

It was pissing down about seven years later. Beanz was now seventy. Buster anxiously barked at the front door, got up on his back legs and scratched at it, wanting to get out.

'Righto, little mate, I hear ya.'

Beanz opened the front door a little, enough to let Buster out into the wind and rain for a piss. There was a young lady standing there, about to knock on the door. She had in hand a tiny dog that lay in the crook of her arm. Buster was keen to check the little fella out.

'Shit!' Beanz said, a little surprised to see somebody there. 'I got a fright then.'

The young women reckoned, 'G'day.'

'G'day. How can I help you, young lady?' he asked politely. The girl looked to be in her thirties. Beanz realised she was probably one of his many ex-student friends come to find some long-lost fellow student, visit or say hello. Thankful students had made time to drop in on the ever-fascinating Professor Beanz. The young lady stood silent and looked deeply into Beanz's face. The young woman smiled when she recognised Beanz's eyes. Then the stranger spoke.

'It is you? My Old Beanz.'

Beanz laughed and laughed as he widened the door.

Frankie had received a similar package in the mail after Luce's death. A hand-written note and one hundred and fifty thousand dollars.

The note read, 'I will miss you, my fine friend.'

Frankie had retired from surgery long ago. She used the money Luce gave her and her entire savings to open her own little restaurant in Sydney. It was very successful. She was nearly eighty, but her Chinese complexion looked twenty years younger. Still beautiful, still independent and even sharper than her favourite scalpel. Her legally recognised husband had died six years ago. She still travelled to Cairns once or twice a year to visit old Beanz and keep her isolation at bay. Since her retirement she had spent a lot of time remembering the time she had spent with Luce. She wished they could have been together longer. One bright day a car pulled up her driveway and her female Jack Russell, Mai Mai, was excited to see two little similar dog faces among some fishing rods in the backseat window of the stranger's car, wagging their mischievous tails. Beanz stepped out from the car with a young women Frankie did not recognise, perhaps thirty years old.

Frankie teased, 'What are you doing here, Beanz, in that old bomb?'

His car was an old petrol-powered Ford station wagon. Frankie and Beanz hugged and greeted each other with huge smiles.

'We have come to visit. And the old bomb still runs great, thank you very much. I don't like those electric bastards. They're too small and bloody gutless.'

The stranger wasn't beautiful to Frankie's eye but there was something strikingly handsome and familiar about her. Something rough, indelicate and recognisable. The girl smiled at Frankie. Frankie became intrigued. 'I thought I knew that dog for a moment then, Beanz ... He almost looks like ...?' It was just like Rexxie.

She had to ask, 'Who is this child, Beanz? Your long-lost granddaughter?'

'This, Frankie, is Lucy.'

The two girls stared into each other's eyes. Lucy's eyes had the beginnings of tears.

'I know those eyes, Lucy.'

The young woman spoke. 'How I have missed you, my fine friend.'

Frankie's shoulders jolted back as she let the words sink in.

Beanz interrupted, 'Go get some clothes, woman. We're on holidays!'

The three embraced and laughed loudly. Frankie picked up an excited Rex, hugging and kissing him furiously. 'Little Rexxie!' He was the proud runt of his new litter of furry friends when Frankie returned 'The King of Runts' to his tiny feet for a quick round of dog bonding and intense bum sniffing.

'Come inside, you lot. Help yourselves to whatever. Just give me a minute, eh?'

Frankie livened up and quick-stepped through to the bedroom and packed her essentials. Then she raided a well-stocked fridge to fill a large Esky and left, locking her empty house.

Lucy walked happily, smiling arm in arm between her two elderly friends towards the waiting car.

Three little dogs, Rexxie, Buster and Mai Mai eagerly followed.

-The End-

GLOSSARY = WHAT SHIT MEANS . . .

Acid = LSD

Ambo = ambulance bearer = paramedic

Barra = barramundi, legendary chromed fish.

Bead = to see or aim

Beak = a judge

Bikes = biker gangs

Blast = a shot = an injection

Bogan = yobbo = mungbean = redneck

Bon and Malcolm = rock and roll royalty = look them up

Boo = weed = junga = gunga = cannibis = pot = smoke = smoko = herb

Brace and bits = got the shits

Brute = deodorant used by old men

Bucket bongs = bunger = joint = billy = bong = cone = paraphenalia = i'm sure you're catching on

Buckley's = you got fuck all chance. Eg, ya got fuck'n buckleys of living jumping off that ten storey building

Bull = mate eg G'day Bull

Bullocky = bullock team driver

Bully man = see police

Bungee = mate

Busting his ring = work'n hard

Cabbage and eggplant = Brain damaged / brain injury

Cack'n ya dacks = pack'n ya dacks = shat or shitting yourself (see also skidmarks)

Captain Cook = to have a look

Cheesy flick = shithouse movie

Chico roll = Aussie pastry

Chuck a whitie = freaking out = passing out

Coeys = co-accused = five-eighth

Cold pies = trouble

Come a gutser = to fall

Cooch = lawn grass or vagina

Cricket = a ball game that requires a shitload of alcohol to play and watch properly

Crook = sick

Dead horse = rhyming slang for tomato sauce

Dice'n me? = you avoiding me?

Dish pig = kitchen hand / dish washer

Divied up = divided up

Dodgy = bad

Dog it = yellow = to be a coward, low down maggot

Dog's eye = rhyming slang for pie. eg Would you like some dead horse on your dog's eye?

Double dutch = two ropes skipping

Dreamtime = look into it

Duke(s) = fist(s)

Dunny = Shit house = toilet

Durry = dart = cigarette

Egg beater = Fishing reel

Elbow = pound

Esky's = ice box = cooler

Fair whack = see lagin

Fart arse'n = fuck'n round

Federallies = police = bully man = oink = pigs = fucking cops

Fits = needles = picks

Forty pounder = forty ounce bottle of alcohol

Frangers = condoms

Freckle = bum hole

Game of sticks = pool = eight ball

Gammon = to be useless, for something to be shit, even being too proud of yourself. Can also be gammon if you're an arsey bugger

Gander = to look = squizz = clock

Go commando = commando = bugs' balls free of restraint = freeballing

Go'e = speed = meth anphetamine = whipper

Goona = shit

Gray Nic = gray nicholls = a brand of cricket bat

Grunter = good eating fish, grunts like a pig

Gutchy = fucked, rooted

Hard top = coupe = two door = Aussie beast of a fuck'n thing.

Henry Lawson = legendary Australian bush poet

Hill's hoist = Aussie invented, revolving clothes line

Homo non-cryus = a variety of men who can't cry

Hooker = Rugby League front row playing position

Hoyk = chuck = throw

Jackie-jackie = someone who does it all for ya

Jocks = undies

Junk = heroin

Kicker = motorbike's kick starter

Knocked me drink over = skull ya drink

Lagin or lag'n = time inprisoned. A big lag'n usually five years and over.

Little lag'n = under that

Landy = landrover

Lawyer cane = the cuts = long rod

Main drag = main street = main h'way

Mallee scrub = a type of jungle

Mickey bull = cleanskin = a wild uncivilised unbranded beast or bull. Can't eat them if their skin is branded. No brand = fresh beef

Migaloo = white bloke

Mouthpiece = lawyer

Mugs away = looser of eight ball has to set em up

Munted = really fucked up, messed up

Nah, yeah = no

Noggin = your head = ya scone

Old Spice = deodorant for old men

Orchy Bottle = plastic orange juice container perfect for making hand bongs

Over the pits = roadworthy

Pannikin = traditional Aussie, unbreakable tin cup

Pick = needle

Poison rope = snake

Queenslander = a house style usually two storey timber

Quincans = Australian Aboriginal bad spirits

Righto = OK

Red back = venomous Australian spider

Rock-spider = maggot paedoephile = prison's lowest denominator

Screws = screw dog cunts = prison wardens

Seppo = yank = septic tank = seppo = an American

Six cuts = see lawyer cane

Skidmarks = brown stuff you'll find on bugs' jocks if he ever bloody wore any

Skint = broke

Snappy saurus = big lizards = old, giant bloody crocs

Stick magazines = Playboy, Penthouse

Stir = jail

Sour crack = Mary's bum hole

The Old Victa = Australian lawn mower

Three on the tree = column shift three speed gear box

Thunk = what someone thunks he thought

Top end = Northern Australia

Towey = shitty = having your rags

Up the Rudder = up the arse

V.D. = S.T.D. = venereal disease = the herp

VB song = Aussie beer song on tv

Wag school = cut school = take the day off school

Warm Beer = trouble

Watch house = police lock up

Werewolf ya = creep up on you

White Ox = rolling tobacco and common tender in prison

Without a stitch = naked

XXXX = Queensland beer, same colour as horse piss

Yeah, nah = yeah

Yonks = a long time

Z900 = Kwacca nine = The Z = Kawasaki Z900 road bike

ACKNOWLEDGEMENTS

Thank you to everyone.

R.H. Croll, Motley Crue, ACDC, John Bonham, Phil Rudd, Jimmy Page, Jimmy Hendrix, Angus Young, Malcolm Young, Bon Scott, Bob Marley, Led Zeppelin, Mozart, Ten, Susanne, Philip, Georgie the podcaster, Jim Beam, Jack Daniels, Wild Turkey and The Noble Weed.

My dogs past and present: Pachuko, King George, Rexxie, Buster, King Louis, Ziggy, Zoe, Rosie, Boof, Buddy and Holly. The unforgettable and chaotic Pig Pig. So much happiness, so much laughter. See you all again under our bridge.

Cover art by Robert Scholten.

CONNECT WITH ME:

📷 *Robert.Lee.Johnston*

🐦 *@R_L_Johnston*

📘 *Author Robert Lee*

Johnston

Check out my podcast:
http://www.buzzsprout.com/182351